A GIFT IN THE SUNLIGHT

An Armenian Story

A Novel

by

Kay Mouradian

*To Bruce and Donna
Friends from Snow Country
all the Best
Kay Mouradian*

Taderon Press
London and Reading

COVER CREDIT: Apples From Heaven - The Armenian Alphabet by John T. Ventimiglia donated to Mt. Holyoke College, South Hadley MA by Annette V. Terzian in memory of Ebraxé Momjian Terzian, Teacher.

Published by Taderon Press, PO Box 2735, Reading RG4 8GF, England.

Printed in association with the Gomidas Institute.

2005   5 4 3 2 1

ISBN 1-903656-56-7

DISTRIBUTED WORLDWIDE:
Garod Books Ltd.
42 Blythe Rd.
London, W14 0HA
Email: *info@garodbooks.com*

TABLE OF CONTENTS

AUTHOR'S NOTE

While growing up as an American kid in Boston, my mother, Flora, would tell me stories about her own childhood in Turkey. A survivor of the Armenian genocide, her heartrending stories became the basis for this novel. But I would not have written this book at all if it hadn't been for a series of remarkable incidents that happened to my mother in her last years.

Flora's life had been colored by the horrors of the genocide. Steeped in anger and self-pity, she constantly mourned the loss of her family who had perished at the hands of the Turks. But in her last years, through a series of near-death experiences, the shadows of the past began to part. Something was happening inside Flora's heart, something beyond my ability to understand. The old bitterness was gone, and the unconditional love buried deep in her heart was set free. Everyone around her felt it. She was fragrant with love, like a flower releasing its perfume for all to enjoy.

As she emerged from her second near death-experience, she told me in no uncertain terms that I was going to write a book about her life. I resisted the idea. I was in the midst of researching materials for an entirely different book. But what was happening to my elderly mother was so unusual and so wonderful that I decided to give serious thought to what she had said on that prophetic night in cardiac care.

I began to read about events that happened in the Ottoman Empire during World War I and became overwhelmed. I began to understand the scars on my mother's heart and on the hearts of Armenian survivors everywhere. Now I knew that my mother's story needed to be told—the whole of it, including the blessing that was granted her at the end of her life to see into the depths of life and be transformed.

This is more than just Flora's story. It is also the story of every Armenian who survived that tragic historical event that continues to be glossed over by the modern world.

ACKNOWLEDGEMENTS

There are many individuals I'd like to thank for their interest, encouragement and editorial suggestions. Especially to Cathy Dees and to the late Kay Croissant, whose hope and inspiration kept me writing when I'd rather have been playing tennis. Their editorial suggestions were vital to the development of this heartrending story. Without their continual encouragement I would never have started or finished this work.

To Joyce Engleson, Sonia Massie, Linda Hudson and Gary Goshgarian for their professional advice.

To my writing peers, Sandy Statdler, Holly Lee Vecchio, Maggie Malooly, Jim Schliedge, Jay Brakensick, Kathi Henry, Ralph Pray, Mike Mayock and Joellen Murphy, I extend my gratitude for your years of patience in listening to all those chapter changes.

To the late Anna Hovanesian and Taline Anderson for translating letters written in ancient Turkish Armenian and to the late Garabed Aaronian whose eyewitness accounts in his unpublished memoir revealed treasured insights.

To those of you who asked to read early drafts of the manuscript and whose heartfelt responses said this story held promise I thank Anne Ananosian, Maggie Bedrosian, Arlene Aaronian, Peggy Hamlin, Aida and Edmund Bedrosian, Michele Froelick, Dina Chalakian, Gertrude Straede, Haik Hagopian, Janet Dunn, Diane Vinson, Tillie Rounds, Lili Balian, Paul and Rosemary Kalemkarian, Tiiu Harunk, Ann Patterson, Hugh and Petrie Wilson and especially to Jack Bournazian and Jim Ajemian.

To Steve Bedrosian and Eiko Amano for their computer savvy suggestions and to my cheerleader friends, Armen Aroyan and Chuck and Victoria Gevoian, who prodded me and never let me forget that this story needed to be published.

To Ara Sarafian who sensed the determined energy and depth of the wound behind this story and published it.

And to Flora... who taught me *what life is all about.*

MAP OF THE OTTOMAN EMPIRE, 1915
SHOWING HISTORIC WESTERN ARMENIA, CILICIAN ARMENIA
AND MODERN TURKEY

Caspian Sea

RUSSIAN EMPIRE

Historic
Western Armenia

Black Sea

OTTOMAN EMPIRE

DESERT OF ZOR

Der Zor

Syria

Hadjin

Aleppo

Adana

Cilician
Armenia

Constantinople

Modern Turkey

Mediterranean Sea

Smyrna

GREECE

CHAPTER ONE

THE PROCLAMATION

May 19, 1915. Hadjin, Turkey

War was singeing the edges of Turkey. Six months had passed since Turkey joined Germany and Austria in the Great War, but in the isolated mountain town of Hadjin life had not much changed. The winter snows had melted, dirt roads were soft and muddy from an early spring thaw, dogs and cats roamed Hadjin's hilly streets and the days were peaceful. Old men still met in coffeehouses, their exuberant voices ringing as they tossed dice on backgammon boards calling out *shesh besh*.

Sitting across from his business partner in the local coffeehouse, Hagop Munushian scratched at his graying mustache, adjusted the red fez that covered his bald head, tossed the dice on his pearl inlaid board and quickly moved his white pieces. He smiled, thinking he was about to win the game.

Sipping Turkish coffee from a chipped demitasse, he glanced out the sooty window to watch the comings and goings in the Armenian town he loved. Women in long dresses sauntered from shop to shop as young girls filled water jugs at the old stone fountain in the center of the square. And then he saw her, his daughter Flora entering the square. Wiry, small and skinny, her long, brown pigtails slapping against the empty leather water bag strapped to her back, she was walking briskly toward the fountain. She was a whirlwind of energy, always in a hurry. Hagop tried not to favor any of his children, but Flora, his fourth child, carried a special place in his heart.

He looked beyond the scene, upward to the huge American missionary compound where Flora attended school. The site dominated the rockbound picturesque plateau, with its backdrop of the majestic, craggy Taurus Mountains jutting high into the sky. Those were his mountains, where as a young boy he had hiked with his father. Now he was the father caring for his family and teaching his own children about life.

He had a summer home and a vineyard in those mountains, a refuge from his smelly, dirty, but profitable, tanning business. Summers were his delight, high in the sweet air with his wife and mother, his five sons and two daughters. Summers were happy times, and six weeks from now he and his family would be in those mountains working the vineyard—picking and drying grapes into raisins, storing packs of salted leaves for the winter months and drying grape juice into a sweet tasting fruit leather.

He smiled, thinking of his children crushing the grapes for wine, purple-footed and making a silly game of it. Scamps, every one of them, except for Verkin, his beautiful elder daughter who had a kind of womanly dignity that kept her aloof from childplay. She was very different from Flora who stomped on the grapes with gusto, always trying to out do her brothers.

Flora did not come into the world easily. Five weeks premature, she almost did not survive. It was in the first year of the twentieth century, on the sixth of September, when she was born.

His mother, Shushan, had delivered the new addition to his growing family. "A vision," she had said, her eyes widening as she handed him his newest daughter. "I see many gifts coming to this child, some in the sunlight and some in the shadow, all showering down from heaven."

Having heard his mother's prophecies many times before, Hagop smiled. He wrapped a blanket around his tiny daughter and handed the swaddled infant to his wife, into her outstretched arms. "She's frail, Arpi," he said, "like a delicate flower."

Arpi placed her new daughter to her breast. "Flora. We should call her Flora."

Minutes later, Hagop, with his huge hands, tenderly took the infant, pressed little Flora to his heart, and sang her a song.

Don't be afraid, my sweet little Flora.

Father is here and you will grow strong.

In the days that followed, Arpi's milk ceased to flow. Hagop's mother, who understood the healing ways, said, "*Nour*, pomegranates. The child needs juice from pomegranates."

As if lovingly tending to a sick bird, Hagop had fed his tiny daughter drops of an elixir he had made from pomegranates. It saved her life.

His pleasant reverie abruptly ended. Dust spiraled upward as a soldier on horseback galloped into the square. Hagop watched warily as the soldier pulled up short in front of the bakery. Turkish soldiers were a common sight lately, but there was something about this one....

The Turk dismounted and strutted toward the small wood-frame building. Clutching a hammer and a sheaf of paper, he nailed a notice to the wall, remounted and kicked up more dust as he sped away.

"Something's happening!" Hagop yelled and bolted out the door. A dozen eyes followed him. Chairs screeched and backgammon boards flew. Everyone in the square was rushing toward the bakery.

Hagop raced past them and felt his heart sink when he saw the large type. He scanned the notice and two sentences leapt out at him:

ATTENTION ALL ARMENIANS
ALL ARMENIANS WILL BE MOVED TO THE INTERIOR UNDER ESCORT OF THE TURKISH ARMY.

ALL ARMENIANS MUST BE PREPARED TO LEAVE WITHIN FIVE DAYS. PERSONS WHO AID OR SHELTER OR GIVE FOOD TO THE ARMENIANS WILL BE SENT BEFORE COURT MARTIAL FOR EXECUTION.

There was much, much more. The bold, angry words momentarily paralyzed him. He could hardly breathe. He looked at the ashen faces around him and saw shock, disbelief and panic. Racing toward Flora, he grasped her hand and saw the fear in her eyes. He lifted his head and pleaded to the heavens. "God... help us all."

The war had come to Hadjin.

CHAPTER TWO

THE FIRST DAY

Hagop opened the front door of his home. Soldiers were everywhere.

"Be at the bridge at seven in the morning," a soldier shouted and rushed by.

His face expressionless, Hagop closed the door and leaned against it. He swallowed the lump in his throat and tightened his fists. Five agonizing days had passed since the posting of the relocation notice. "Relocate, deport, transfer. Damn! Those words all mean the same thing," he snarled. His family and every other Armenian in the Ottoman Empire were being forced out of their homes and driven from their homeland.

Every family was struggling. What to take? Letters? Photographs? Books? Food? Water? Mattresses? Blankets? Only what they could carry…that's what the Turkish proclamation said. As difficult as it was, Hagop was ready.

The next morning, his face strained, Hagop gathered his family in front of his home and studied their faces. His second son, Levon, eighteen years old, his mustache sprouting, had high hopes of studying medicine in Paris. But Hagop worried the Turks would draft him into their army as they did his eldest, Antranig. After serving for two years, Antranig managed to desert, found his way to Egypt and was now on the high seas, on a freighter on its way to America. Hagop was grateful his eldest wouldn't be subjected to the hell he knew was ahead for the rest of his family.

He placed his hand on the shoulder of his beautiful Verkin, sixteen and resplendent. With her long, shiny auburn hair and her sky blue eyes, his friends said she was the prettiest girl in Hadjin. Years ago Hagop and Armen Avakian's father had agreed their children would one day marry. Verkin's engagement ceremony had been planned for this summer. Another dream the war had crushed. Then there was his feisty, hazel eyed fourteen-year old Flora, who some called *Nourji*, because his pomegranate elixir had saved her life. Last summer Flora had spent a month of study in Constantinople with American missionaries. Her scholastic ambitions made him uneasy. She was unlike other girls in Hadjin whose primary goal was to marry and have children.

His son Toros had just turned eleven, his face a mirror of his elder sister. The youngster loved to spend time with him in his warehouse. He was the son Hagop thought would one day take over his business. Standing behind Toros was six-year-old Dickran, his dark hair sticking straight up. Dikran never combed his hair and would run and hide if he saw one of his sisters approaching with a comb.

His dear wife Arpi clutched their youngest, three year old Avedis, against her breasts, as if she feared losing him. She had cried herself to sleep the last five nights, and her swollen eyes were a testament of her grief. His attempts to console her had been futile, and he wondered if his feeling of helplessness had fueled her fears. Then there was his mother, Shushan, who had been praying constantly, pleading to her God for a reprieve. She was approaching seventy. His most immediate concern was for her. How would she fare?

Not uttering a word, he went back inside his home. His eyes wandered to the cradle he had made for his babies, the marriage bed of his parents, the books Flora and Levon loved. He picked up the family Bible, kissed it and read the page where he had recorded the births of his children. He lifted a floorboard to hide it and to his surprise he saw Flora's diary. Picking it up, he opened it, but immediately closed it, respecting his daughter's privacy. His heart ached. Would those pages deteriorate along with his scholarly daughter's hopes? He carefully placed his Bible beside the diary and prayed that he and his family would return safely. Replacing the floorboard, he made the sign of the cross, took one long last look, and locked the door behind him.

He tallied the food in the cart attached to *Esh,* his donkey. His hand lingered on a sack of raisins. Drying those grapes, crushing others for wine, picking, salting and storing the grape leaves…his simple summer home at his vineyard high in the mountains… those memories flooded over him. *Damn Turks! May they rot in Hell!*

"Let's go," he said, following other families who had already started down the hill. As far as he could see, people from all sides of town were gathering by the river's edge. No one talked. The air was heavy with fear. Shuffling feet, braying donkeys and squeaky wheels were the only sounds heard.

Hagop felt the knot in his stomach tighten as he passed the warehouse he had built twenty years ago. He glanced at the lock on the double doors. Piles of camel, bear and sheepskins he owned will be gone when *and if* he ever returned to his beloved Hadjin. He knew the Turks would break through the doors and like thieves in the night confiscate his treasures, his hard work.

"Hagop," a familiar voice called out. It was Nubar, his business partner.

"My donkey is loaded," Nubar said. "I took two camel skins and hated leaving the others behind. Those damn Turks will steal them, I know."

Hatred poured through Hagop's dark eyes, a chill running up his spine. But as he approached the edge of town, he felt a ray of hope. There, waiting by the river, was a familiar face among the eight Turkish soldiers on horses. The officer in charge was Captain Khourshid. Hagop remembered that day when the captain, writhing in pain, was brought to his mother, whose reputation as a healer was well known. His mother held the captain's mangled leg, manipulated his ankle and toes, gently reset the broken bone, plastered the tender area with comfrey, and braced the leg with a splint. The grateful captain, bathed in relief, wanted to pay her, but Shushan refused the money.

He watched the captain lead some of his soldiers across the aged wooden bridge. The clatter of horses' hoofs reverberated like a wailing echo. Then, as if on cue, the sounds ceased, almost as if time had stopped. The silence was eerie as the soldiers sat upright, waiting.

No one wanted to cross that bridge. Then, hesitantly, an anguished soul took that reluctant step. The march had begun. Minutes felt like hours before Hagop and his family reached the bridge. More than a hundred persons were ahead and hundreds more were behind. Hagop looked with envy at the rushing water as it splashed against the rocks and boulders as the river drove the sweet water flowing down from the mountain streams. *It's just another day in the life of the river,* he thought, and wished his own life could be as normal. But that was not to be. He was on the brink of the unknown, on the edge of a precipice. He held onto the railing and noticed Flora staring back at her school. "Come, Flora! We must not look back." His heart felt heavy. He needed to heed his own words.

* * *

Once filled with life and energy, the Protestant missionary school atop Hadjin's highest plateau now cast a desolate and haunting aura. That's how Flora felt. Empty. Learning was the spark in her life and now, as she looked up at the American missionary compound, she longed to be there—with her teachers, her friends and her books. Slamming her foot against the bridge, she turned to see the same anger and pain written on the faces of the hundreds lined up and waiting.

Harried men tried to keep their families and animals together. Old men and women were tight with despair. Children were befuddled. Bewildered mothers, especially those whose breasts were heavy with milk, gripped their infants. Pregnant women held their bellies, alarm written on their faces. Flora wanted to comfort Mrs. Albarian who looked as if her baby was ready to be birthed.

This was a day she'd never forget. All they had was what they could carry, and they clutched the few possessions they dared take. They were leaving their homes and their way of life. Their hopes and dreams were fading too. That unforgettable moment, caught in a glimpse, was pushed into the recesses of Flora's mind, to be seared there forever.s

What privacy will any of us have, she wanted to shout. *Will Mrs. Albarian and all those other pregnant women have to deliver their babies by the side of the road?* She, too, was feeling distressed. And embarrassed. Her menstruation had started early that morning. Where will she be able to change her soiled cloth?

When her feet touched the soft soil on the other side of the river, she turned for one last look, but moisture in her eyes blurred her vision. The memory of the last time she had crossed this bridge flooded over her. It was nearly a year ago when her favorite teacher, Miss Webb, had arranged for Flora and her two friends, Ana and Sona, to attend a summer of study at the American College for Girls in Constantinople. Constantinople had triggered her spirit of adventure. Exciting. That's how Flora remembered it. Her hopes had soared. America. Miss Webb suggested she should think about studying in America. Now that dream was crumbling.

Her sister, walking alongside her, hadn't said a word. Verkin, too, felt miserable, but tried to mask her grief. Against her mother's wishes, Verkin insisted on wearing her favorite green linen dress. Verkin loved pretty clothes and she looked wonderful, even on this dreaded day. Flora wanted to say something, but couldn't find the right words. Then she heard her three-year-old brother's squeaky voice. Avedis, with his little arms stretched out, ran, and jumped into her arms. Lowering him to the ground, she held his tiny hand until the march became too strenuous. Then she and Verkin took turns carrying the little fellow.

Three hours later two soldiers on horses approached, indicating a rest break. As one of the soldiers pointed to the river that followed the road, his eyes lingered on a pretty teenage girl. Flora recognized him. *His facial birthmark.* Quivering, she recalled that terrible day when he and the other soldier had ransacked her home. She bolted, her sister right on her heels. They lit out toward their brother, Levon, who was tying their donkey to a tree by the river.

"I'm going to help grandmother. Stay with Esh," he yelled to them.

They watched him rushing back to the congested road. He stopped and said something to Avedis, who was running toward Flora as fast as his little legs would go.

Flora kept her eyes focused on the two Turkish soldiers. They unnerved her. Sex was not a subject she knew a lot about, and she was not all that experienced in the world, but she knew those two soldiers were to be feared. She clasped her sister's hand, and relief flooded over both of them when the two soldiers rode away. There was no need for words. They understood the danger.

Just three days ago those two soldiers had forced their way into her home. That day was still etched in Flora's mind. "Search!" the soldier had screamed as he slammed through the front door and shoved Levon aside. He marched in and a second soldier followed him, his face exactly like the first, except for a huge birthmark. It covered most of his left cheek and part of his forehead and chin. "Stay where I can see you!" he shouted. "Sit on the bench against the wall," he ordered. Her little brother's scream pierced the room. "Quiet him!" the soldier demanded. Trembling, her mother yanked Avedis onto her lap, shushing and rocking him until his wailing stopped.

Terrified, the family sat together watching the soldiers tear through their home, snatching the rifle off the wall, overturning shelves and drawers and dumping everything on the floor, turning over their beds, and pulling out every book in the bookcase, leafing through the pages and hurling them at the wall. The first soldier came out of the kitchen carrying all the knives, including her father's trimming knife. It was his favorite, his vital tool, his livelihood. Her father leaped from the bench and lunged at the soldier. "My knife!"

"Get away!" The soldier with the birthmark rammed the butt of the rifle into her father's chest, and he crumpled to the floor. Shoving his foot into the middle of her father's back, he said, "Stay in your house. You'll be told when to leave Hadjin." His eyes fell on Verkin, lingering on her rounded breasts.

"We don't have time for that now," the first soldier had lashed out, and they stormed through the opened door. Flora remembered racing to bolt the door shut, to shut them out of their lives forever.

And now they were back. What to do? Tell her parents…who had no weapons to protect them? *No*, she decided, *not yet*. This day was difficult enough. And as long as Captain Khourshid was among them, she knew she and her sister would be safe. Last summer Captain Khourshid had escorted her, Miss Webb, and Flora's friends to Constantinople and then back to Hadjin. The captain was kind and noble.

The donkey brayed. Flora patted his rump and sat under the tree where he was tied and watched Verkin join scores of others already at the water's edge. Avedis plopped himself next to her, resting his head in her lap.

"Tell me a story, Flora," Avedis's playfulness suggesting he was on a picnic rather than a forced march. "Tell me the story about the dervish," he said, snuggling up a bit more and putting his thumb in his mouth.

Wanting to protect him from the reality of the day, Flora said, "So that's the one you want to hear. All right." She stretched her legs and said, *"A long time ago there was and was not in ancient Armenia a wicked dervish and an innocent young lad, and his name was Avedis... just like yours."* She kissed him on the cheek. *"One day,"* she continued, *"the dervish caught Avedis and stuffed him into a large sack...."*

Avedis, his thumb slipping out of his mouth, fell fast asleep. Flora cradled her arm around him. She recalled her own joy when she was little like her brother and Grandmother Shushan, the real storyteller in the family, had transported her into a world of magic, mystery, goodness and love. She longed for that joyful peace to be back in her life.

* * *

As the family gathered together under the tree, Flora's father handed everyone only a few raisins. "We must be careful with the food," he said. "We have no idea how long we will be gone."

Flora chewed her share slowly, one raisin at a time, wanting the sweet taste to last as long as possible. She was hungry, but wouldn't complain, and neither did anyone else in the family. Flora wanted to stay under the umbrella of the shady tree and pretend this day was nothing more than a family day by the river. But as people began to stumble back to the road that was taking them away from everything they knew, the bubble of her pretense burst. Not so for Avedis, however. He ran to the road and yelled, "Flora, come and catch me." Reluctantly she raced to him, encircled her arms around his waist, twirled him and set him down. Avedis ran through the maze of people and came back to Flora, laughing and making a game of it.

Then as the afternoon progressed, they fell into the lethargic rhythm of the march. Distances grew between clusters of people. The old began to falter. Flora looked for her grandmother and saw her in the distance. Nubar was still with her. Wonderful Nubar. He was always considerate of her family. He had even offered to help fund Levon's medical education in Paris, but the damn Turks had quashed her brother's dream as well as her own.

As the sun dipped toward the horizon, the convoy reached the outskirts of Feke, a Turkish village where they were to camp for the night. The ground was already choked with families settling for a small space on which to rest their weary bodies. Flora saw her father, mother and Verkin clearing rocks from the ground that was to be her home for the evening and night.

"Avedis," her father yelled as he placed the rocks into a circle, "go help Dickran and Toros find small pieces of wood for a fire." The youngster ran to join his two brothers who were racing back and forth to their father with as much wood their small arms could carry, struggling to outmaneuver others who were also scavenging for firewood.

"Where's Levon?" Flora asked.

"At the river. Getting water."

"I'm going there too," she said, wondering if she'd find any privacy to wash her menstrual cloth. She wandered through a maze of people fetching water and found Levon, who had already filled the family's leather water bag. She stood next to him. Together they watched huge rapids swirl over rocks, boulders and trees propelling the thundering water down into a steep and rocky gorge.

A huge trout jumped out of river and dove back in. "Would be nice for dinner," Levon said, and the fish jumped again, right in front of them. Levon lunged for it, lost his footing and found himself sprawled on the riverbank.

"Levon! You could have been pulled into the gorge!"

He was visibly shaken.

Flora put her hand on her brother's shoulder. "It's not worth your life, no matter how little food we have." Her brother did not respond, but his face was ashen. "Wait for me, Levon. I need to wash something." She left Levon sitting by the riverbank, went up river, found a place where the water was tranquil and disappeared behind two large boulders. After washing her cloth, she returned to see Levon struggling to hold onto a large fish in his hands. A man with a bucket sloshing with water rushed to her brother's side. Levon yelped and tossed the flailing fish into it.

"You won't believe this Flora," he said. "I was sitting there at the riverbank, and this fish swam up to me, and I hit and stunned him with this stick." He grinned and pointed the broken tree branch lying on the ground. "It has to weigh at least seven pounds!" Levon thanked the man for the loan of his bucket and said he'd return it promptly.

They walked back toward the campsite, and as they neared the road, Flora saw her. Grandmother was struggling, Nubar's arm locked into hers. "I'm going to help Grandmother," Flora said and rushed down the road. She held Grandmother Shushan's other arm as she led her and Nubar to the family site.

Too tired to talk, Shushan slumped onto a blanket. Her face was lined with exhaustion. Flora slipped off Grandmother's shoes and gently held her swollen feet. Grandmother winced and laid herself down. Flora gently massaged Grandmother's legs.

The fire crackled as it singed the skin of the trout the family would share at dinner. This was the first day of the forced march and the first day Flora felt the pain of hunger. If this had been a family picnic with plenty of food, it would be joyful sitting around the fire and praising Levon for his prized catch. But they, along with every Armenian in Turkey, now had to live, eat and sleep in the outdoors with all its threatening elements until the Turks said they could go back home. And they had no idea how long that would be.

"I don't like it here anymore," Avedis said to his mother. His face began to pucker, as if he was about to unleash a howl.

Grandmother Shushan, sitting with Avedis and Dikran, lifted Avedis onto her lap and smothered his face with kisses. "Storytime?" The youngster's face was still scrunched and with mournful eyes he sniffed a couple of times and wrapped his arms around her, hugging her for dear life. Cradling him, she kissed the top of his head, smiled and said, "Dikran, come closer." She pulled the six year old to her, and with her soft, gentle voice began their favorite fable. "*A long time ago there was and was not an Armenian king who had three sons who he felt should marry,*" she said. "*He sent each of the boys to different places far, far away to find the perfect girl who could give birth to boys as wonderful as the two of you.....*" Dikran giggled and then Avedis added a complaisant giggle to his brother's happy sound.

Flora, too, listened. She watched her two brothers becoming enthralled with the story, but when Grandmother finished the tale with the traditional, *And three apples fell from heaven,* her grandmother's prophetic eyes dimmed. Shock splashed across Shushan's face, as if someone had struck her with the butt of a rifle. Dazed, she set Avedis down and said, "*And a long time ago there was and was not an Armenia in Turkey.*"

Flora noticed a tear sliding down Grandmother's face. Had the vision been painful? She dared not ask, but she wanted to hold and comfort her, as Grandmother had done to so many. People said Grandmother Shushan had second sight, and some said Shushan could see into the future. All Flora knew was that her grandmother was wise, that people listened to her, and often people came to her about their problems, and sometimes grandmother would put her hands on some part of their body and they would instantly feel better. Flora wished she could do something but knew that Grandmother needed to be quiet and left alone when a vision was painful.

As the sun fell behind the mountain peaks, Flora's father fueled the fire, adding to the orange glow of other campfires. Sparks snapped and flew up into the darkening sky. Nubar and her father spread out the camel skins, a thin folding mattress for Grandmother Shushan, and blankets near the hot coals. The sound of water plunging down the gorge magnified as the quiet of the evening fell.

Sharing a blanket with her sister, Flora wondered what fate had brought her to this disaster, when she felt a hand reach out and touch her. It was Grandmother whispering "Try not to despair, my child. You've had many gifts in the sunlight, and when you think there is only darkness ahead, there can be gifts hidden in those shadows."

"What do you mean, grandmother?"

"We must try to understand why difficult things happen and learn the lessons they bring."

"But I don't understand."

"You will one day." Grandmother smiled said no more. Her peaceful face glowed in the light of the campfire.

Flora gazed up into the dark sky. She understood so little, but after all she was only fourteen, even if people said she was bright and smart and had grand ideas, unlike most girls her age. But then not many young girls had traveled to Constantinople as she had. That's where she lived with girls from other cultures who affected her vision of the world. Americans, especially, had influenced her deeply and sparked a desire for her to leave the land of her ancestors to study in America. But convincing her parents to even let her attend the American missionary school had been a monumental task. That was four years ago, when she was only ten years old.

At that time her parents had been suspicious of the missionaries. Their Armenian parish priest had complained that the American Protestants were stealing his flock, but Flora desperately wanted to go to the missionary school. It had taken all of her courage to plead for the American education. She remembered that day four years ago, as if it was yesterday. Standing in front of their home, she had planted her feet and faced her father, telling him she wanted to learn to speak English at the American school. Not realizing she was holding her breath, it suddenly let go in a burst. He didn't say a word, and her heart sank. She didn't dare tell him the real reason; that she felt as if an invisible force was pulling her toward the high plateau where the American school stood like a magic castle inviting her to enter. Feeling like a balloon that had lost all its air, she followed him into the house.

Her grandmother and sister were sitting together on the bench built against the wall. Grandmother Shushan was teaching Verkin how to make single strands of knots into a doily. Flora felt even more exasperated. There was her sister doing exactly what all good Hadjin girls are supposed to do. Learn to embroider, learn to make delicate doilies, cook, and become a good servant to your husband and children. Flora hated all that stuff. She wanted much more from life.

When her father announced that Flora wanted to go to the American school, an eerie, silent moment filled the room. Verkin and Grandmother looked as if they had stopped breathing. Her mother glared at her. There was fire in her eyes. "Are you crazy," she had shouted. "What will my friends say? How can I face the priest on Sunday? I know what he'll say, *Do you want her to become a Protestant!*" Then she blurted out, "*Why can't you be more like your sister!*"

That's when the knot in Flora's stomach tightened. She ran to the bookcase, pulled out the family Bible, put her hand on the tattered cover, promised never to become a Protestant, and placed the Bible against her heart.

Grandmother, who had great influence on the family, gave her father an approving nod, and the next day Flora's father took her to the American school. When she saw the American flag in the middle of the compound, she ran to the flagpole, pointed to waving flag and with a huge smile on her face said, "*that's my magic carpet.*"

The memory of the red, white, and blue flag fluttering in the morning breeze stilled her racing mind, and there on the first day of the forced march she fell asleep on the hard ground.

CHAPTER THREE

REMEMBERING CONSTANTINOPLE

The next afternoon as they rested by a field Flora looked back at the long line of Armenians blending into the horizon. She was overwhelmed with despondency. She wanted her life back… to be near her beloved teacher, Miss Webb, to attend her English class and maybe even study again in Constantinople. Was it nearly a year ago? Yes, last June, just three months before the war broke out.

Suddenly, she was there again, on her way to Constantinople. She could almost feel the monotonous rocking of the old train that had lulled her teacher and her friends into a light sleep. Her diary cupped in her hands, she had turned the pages back to that special day when Miss Webb told her father a missionary scholarship would pay for her to study English at the American College in Constantinople.

> May 17, 1914. As usual, Mother said no, I couldn't go, and Miss Webb told my Father refused the scholarship saying that Hadjin girls never leave home unless they marry. So I couldn't believe it when Father gave his approval. I heard him tell Mother a war was going to break out and if Antranig didn't desert the army, he could be killed and that Antranig needed money to disappear and that I could take the gold coins to him. There was no other way, he said.

"Never take this belt off," her father had told her in a stern voice. "Even sleep with it. There's enough money hidden in it to take Antranig to America." Flora remembered putting her hand on the belt, as if guarding it, when long blasts of the train's whistle announced they'd soon be in Constantinople. She glanced at her friends Ana and Sona sitting opposite her and Miss Webb. They were orphans. Sixteen-year-old Sona Ajamian and her fourteen-year-old sister, Ana, lived at the American orphanage in Hadjin and often performed at the Mission's Sunday concerts, Sona on the piano and

Ana on the violin. Even though the sisters were talented musicians, Flora pitied them, feeling that nothing in the world could be worse than being an orphan.

She remembered Miss Webb's head bobbing slowly to the rhythm of the train's rocking. Miss Webb was her special gift, in the sunlight, as her grandmother had once prophesied. Flora was on that train because of her teacher, and she was anxious for the new adventures awaiting her in the ancient cosmopolitan city. She recalled her amazement as Constantinople first came into view, as if an artist had sketched an outline of the city but couldn't capture it because the paper wasn't large enough to fit it all in. She never imagined a city could be so big. Carriages, men on horseback, carts, oxen, and donkeys laden with goods crowded the busy streets. She marveled at the huge domes, the minarets and the ornate buildings on the hills across the Golden Horn.

Streets and sidewalks were paved. Sounds from outdoor shops—copper beaters hammering, blacksmiths striking and banging, sewing machines stitching—reverberated like noisy, inharmonious musical notes. Horses pranced on the cobblestone streets, their clip-clop ringing with uneven rhythms.

The city was textured with groups of Europeans, Armenians, Greeks and Turks, so different from Hadjin, where the community was all Armenian. The European women looked grand in their big hats, umbrellas and draped skirts. She recalled seeing the horse carriage with four harem ladies sitting inside, their faces covered with beautiful silk veils. Two huge dark brown men dressed in frocks and red fezzes drove the carriage and the sleek horses. Miss Webb said they were eunuchs.

The sound of horses approaching broke Flora's reverie, and she snapped back to the edge of the field, sitting next to her parents. She glanced up the road to see Captain Khourshid escorting a small group. Two were women. *Could it be?* "It's Miss Webb," she shouted and dashed up the road. The two women pulled up their horses and dismounted.

Flora flew into the missionary's arms. "I never thought I'd see you again." Her heart was pounding, and then she recognized the other American missionaries. "Why are you here?"

"Our orphans are in the convoy a day ahead of yours," Miss Webb said, her face pale. "The Lieutenant in charge of our convoy *ordered* us to leave. Said we missionaries had to return to Hadjin."

"Ana and Sona?" Flora asked.

"I left them in charge of the little ones," Miss Webb said, her voice trailing off in obvious distress. Flora knew why. The orphans had no one to watch over them, and Flora's own deep fear of becoming orphaned surfaced. Then she heard the captain's commanding voice call out, "Mr. Munushian!"

The captain handed the reins of a horse to her father. "The mare is old, but still useful," he said. "Your family is large. She'll be of help." Her father took the reins, stood speechless, and followed the captain who was walking his horse toward the missionaries. "I'll send my sergeant to escort you back to Hadjin," he said to Miss Webb and to Mr. and Mrs. Peet, the missionary husband and wife who were accompanying Miss Webb. The Captain acknowledged their gratitude and gently prodded his horse as he rode toward the head of the convoy.

"Thank heavens that kind man is in charge of your convoy," Mr. Peet said.

"Yes indeed," Miss Webb concurred, her voice tinged with anger. She turned abruptly. "Mr. Munushian," she blurted out. "Let me take Flora with me. I'll take her to Constantinople with us."

Hope flashed across Flora's face.

But her father's face darkened. "That's not a good idea," he said. "I don't trust the Turks. They may not let her go with you because she's Armenian. They could send her with another convoy and then who'd protect her?" Hagop reached for Flora's hand. "No, not this time, Miss Webb."

Flora desperately wanted to go. Her hopes and dreams hinged on Miss Webb and her American education. But if the Turks didn't care about the orphans being alone, they could be just as cruel toward her.

She squeezed her father's hand and said, "I must stay with my family."

"Yes, of course. You must. I'm not thinking straight. And I have no idea how we Americans will be treated either." Miss Webb reached into her saddlebag, pulled out her Bible, and handed it to Flora. "Read this every day and think of me." Miss Webb stroked Flora's long hair. "Never give up hope." She gazed deeply into Flora's hazel eyes. "Don't lose your faith. God has given us the opportunity to grow and become as wonderful as He is. Remember that." She kissed the top of Flora's head.

"It's probably a good idea to cut her hair," Miss Webb said to Hagop as she remounted and steadied her horse. Her blue eyes softened, "Remember Flora, always keep hope in your heart."

The horses carried the three Americans away. The road was thick with men and women reaching out to touch them. Flora heard their cries. "Tell America. Tell America to help us. Tell America and *quickly!*" Flora shouted, knowing her plea wouldn't be heard by Miss Webb who was already too far away. As the missionaries faded behind hazy swirling dust, Flora lost sight of them. Her hopeful future was fading with their every stride, and her heart sank.

CHAPTER FOUR

A MISSIONARY'S CREED

"I'll telegraph the American Ambassador," Miss Webb promised as she clasped every hand that reached out to her. She hoped her words might have a calming affect on the frightened people. "Yes, I'll tell America," she said. "Keep God in your hearts. Pray for His guidance, and so will I."

She had been in Turkey for ten years and loved the Hadjin Armenians, especially the ones she knew best, those who attended the Protestant services. She couldn't understand why these peaceful people were being exiled. What terrible deeds had they done? Yes, there had been Armenians in the border town of Van who had welcomed the Russian army into their city and together fought the Turks. But a month later the Turkish army retook Van, and the Van Armenians paid a terrible price—and so did every other Armenian in the empire for the Van rebellion. And yet, Hadjin was so far from the Russian border... how could this remote mountain town be a threat?

If the stars had said Hadjin was her lot in life, she would have believed it. She loved her role as teacher in the American mission. She was a preacher's daughter and wanted to carry on her father's goodness. Had she been born a boy, she would have followed her father's footsteps and become an ordained Congregational minister, but that option was not open to girls. She felt the next best thing was to live a Christian life by helping those less fortunate and she made the choice to leave her comfortable life in Boston to go to a land her father said was in dire need. She had found a home in Hadjin and felt the satisfaction of showing her students a wider world and influencing their young minds with the teachings of Jesus.

But at this moment the pain in her heart was intense. How could the Turks think her orphans could be a threat? She turned for one last look at Flora. It was almost to much too bear. How she had longed to have a daughter, one as bright and feisty as Flora, but that was never to be. Instead she had learned to let *joy* come into her life through students like Flora who were her own dear little sponges soaking up everything she taught.

In that moment she felt as helpless as all the suffering ones who were crying out to her. The cries rang in her soul like an anthem, "Tell America. Tell America." And Miss Webb answered back to every desperate face, "Yes, yes, yes!"

The Lord had given her a new mission.

CHAPTER FIVE

A MOTHER'S WOE

The next morning as the sun rose over the mountain peak, Flora's mother opened her puffy eyes. The ground hard, her feet throbbing, Arpi wanted to shout, "I want my life back... my home! My bed!" Feeling Hagop's heavy breath on the nape of her neck, she knew her husband was still in deep sleep. Had she been home she would have turned and stroked his eyebrows, but at this moment she didn't feel very affectionate. Her eyes welled. *"Enough,"* she said to herself as a salty tear dripped onto her parted lips. Her hands brushed away the wetness, and she vowed she would not cry again. Her family needed her to be strong.

Raising her head, she gazed at her sleeping children. Six-year-old Dickran had rolled off the camel skin he shared with Nubar. Cold, shivering, and feeling like a heavy rock, she laid her head down again. An ominous feeling overwhelmed her. She shot up to a sitting position to look for the mare and the donkey and observed a frenzied man running around masses of sleeping bodies inspecting donkeys. Watching the panicked man, she suspected his animal had been stolen and wondered how many days would pass before her animals would disappear, too. As if her husband had read her direful thought, Hagop sat up, his eyes searching.

"He's still tied to the tree," Arpi said trying to calm him. "The food is safe too." She had insisted they take nothing frivolous, not even toys for the children. Food was their priority. Shushan helped her kill and cook their eight chickens. They packed all the eggs, boiling half of them, and made ample amounts of feta cheese, rice pilav and grape leaves stuffed with onions, raisins and rice. She loaded the cart with items that would last—*basturma* (dried beef), olives, olive oil, bulgur for pilav, raisins, figs, apricots and cherries, both fresh and sun-dried, and cracker bread. Finding bakeries with ovens to bake fresh bread was going to be difficult, but she filled three sacks with flour, anyway. It was painful leaving full barrels of wheat, flour and barley in her cellar—and the wine that Hagop had made from last year's grapes. Had the Turks already stolen them? She visualized Turks in her home as ravenous vultures consuming her food and stealing her treasures. Would her feet ever again sink into her precious Oriental rug? She loved resting her tired body on it, and she longed for it now.

Smelling smoke from nearby campfires, Arpi watched other Armenians awakening to another difficult day on the road. She heard Avedis whining. Shivering and rubbing his eyes, he stumbled over to her and crawled onto her lap. Arpi wrapped her shawl around him and lifted her breast to his mouth. He suckled and when he was satisfied, he said, "Mama. I want to go home."

"Not yet, my sweet."

"I don't like this picnic anymore." Avedis started to cry. "I want to go home."

Arpi smothered him against her breasts and tried but couldn't hold back the tears that streamed down her cheeks.

Avedis raised his head. "Why are you crying, Mother?"

"Because I love you so much," she said, patted his bottom and said, "Go. Your brothers are going to the bushes to relieve themselves." She watched Avedis scramble to keep up with Dickran, who was running to catch up to his two older brothers.

She glanced up the road. Captain Khourshid and two of his soldiers were approaching.

"Morning," the captain said to Hagop.

Arpi watched her husband nod, his eyes saying thank you to the kind captain.

"Time to go," the captain announced.

Arpi didn't want to move. She was not ready for such hardship. Hagop never let her do heavy work. Her job was to care for the children, and her farthest trek was to church every Sunday. She worried how far they'd have to walk today. Her feet were badly blistered.

Then she recognized the two soldiers accompanying Captain Khourshid and shuddered. They were the mean ones who had ransacked her home. The soldier with the birthmark spotted her Verkin, his eyes heavy with desire. Alarmed, Arpi seized her husband's hand.

"Warn the girls," Hagop said with urgency.

Arpi ran to the girls and hovered over them as if protecting them from the devil himself. She watched the soldiers ride on, the one with the birthmark still watching Verkin, a sly smile crossing his face. Blood drained from Arpi's face. She reached into the cart and pulled out a pair of scissors.

"No!" Verkin screamed, tried to get away, but Arpi yanked her arm. Verkin slumped to the ground.

Arpi threw a glance toward Hagop. He nodded, as if to say, *"Now!"*

"No... please... Mother." Verkin pleaded, covering her head with both arms "No. Not my hair!" She began to sob.

"Do you think Armen or any other nice boy will marry you if the soldiers disgrace you?"

"Me, first, Mother," Flora said, wanting to give her sister a little more time. Verkin's shiny, flowing hair was as important to Verkin as the fez was to her bald headed father. Her sister's auburn hair complimented Verkin's smooth, light skin, in direct contrast to most Hadjin girls, who like Flora were olive skinned with dark hair.

Flora felt the familiar pull, as if her mother was going to braid her hair. Suddenly: snip, snip, the wicked nicks sheared off her long hair.

"You're next Verkin," Arpi said.

Verkin reluctantly knelt in front of her mother, her eyes still pleading, as if she hoped to be absolved from an execution. Tears streamed down her cheeks.

Snip, snip, and snip! "There. It's done," Arpi said and took a handful of dirt, smeared both girls' faces and let her muddy hands slide over Verkin's dress. She breathed a sigh of relief.

They were not so pretty anymore.

* * *

That night as the family lay sleeping, Verkin felt a tear roll down her cheek. Angry with her mother, she wanted to run away, maybe back to Hadjin, maybe live with her cousin Siran or with her mother's brother Aram. She knew the thought was absurd. It was dangerous for a pretty young girl to travel alone. There were far too many Turkish soldiers on the move. She shivered, recalling the way the soldier with the ugly birthmark had looked at her, as if he were undressing her with his eyes. She wanted desperately to go back to her peaceful life in Hadjin.

Reaching back to grasp her hair as she had done a thousand times before, her hand fell against her bared neck, her fingers slipping up through scanty strands of hair. Her most beautiful feature was gone. The color and texture of her hair distinguished her from most Armenian girls who, like her sister Flora, had dark hair. Now who would look at her, hover over her and cater to her? Who was she without her shiny auburn hair? She felt as if part of her being had been ripped away. Tears streamed down her cheeks.

It was almost as if her hair had been hallowed, and she knew how to emphasize its natural beauty. She had learned to stretch her neck so her hair would slide across her back and drape over her shoulder just above one of her rounding breasts. And Armen, to whom she was to be betrothed? How would he react if he saw her today? She knew how much he longed to touch and run his fingers through her hair.

Armen. Where is he? Safe in Constantinople? Or has he, too, been deported? Verkin was looking forward to their engagement ceremony. It was to have taken place six weeks from now, at the end of June. That's when Armen was to return home from his first year of dental study in Constantinople. He said he would bring her a gold cross as a betrothal gift, sealing their promise to marry when he finished his schooling and set up a practice in Hadjin. Fortunately, she liked Armen; he was cultured and would one day have a good profession, one that would allow her to buy fine clothes. She had often thought about shopping for a wedding gown, one with a fine, delicate lace that would reveal her long neck and full breasts. She never questioned her father's decision that she would marry Armen.

That's how people married in Hadjin. The fathers decided who would marry whom. Her mother was only thirteen when she married her father, who was twenty-six at the time. They lived with Grandmother Shushan, her mother slept with Grandmother until she turned fifteen, and Verkin was to follow the Armenian marriage tradition. When she married Armen she would live with his parents, but at age eighteen she'd be sleeping with Armen.

Sitting up she pulled the blanket around her shoulders and gazed at her sleeping mother. Grandmother had told Verkin many times that Verkin looked just like her mother when her mother was young. Was she a mirror image of her mother when all the single Armenian men in Hadjin were pursuing her mother? Was that the reason she was her mother's favorite?

Verkin's hands flew to the top of her head and she pulled at her thin and skimpy hair. She knew she should be concerned about her safety and the safety of her family, but at this moment she could only think about the loss of her hair and how she felt like a nobody.

CHAPTER SIX

NOTHING STAYS THE SAME

Flora wasn't sure how she felt about not having long hair anymore. Her head moved more easily and there was no more pull on her scalp, but she had no idea how she looked. Her sister, not yet adjusted to her short hair, pulled the ends of her hair every morning, as if she was trying to lengthen every strand. Verkin did have a different look, but nothing could hide her beauty.

With the days merging into one more tiring day, the memory of meeting Miss Webb was fading. Flora had lost track of how many days had elapsed since that day her beloved teacher rode out of sight. She visualized Miss Webb in her mind every night, talking to her as if her teacher had become a replacement for her diary. She read passages from Miss Webb's Bible every day, but not today. Food was scarce and she hadn't eaten anything solid for two days. She didn't even have enough energy to remove her beloved bible from the cart.

Distances between families were becoming greater and greater. Many were faltering. Today, she and Verkin were among those who lagged behind. Sitting together on the mare, they plodded ahead. Flora turned to look for her ailing grandmother who was on the donkey. Grandmother Shushan, her head drooping, was even farther behind. Flora was losing sight of her father and was becoming nervous. She worried about the two soldiers. Where were they?

CHAPTER SEVEN

THE EVIL AND THE GOOD

The Memoush Oghlou brothers looked alike—skinny, unshaven, dirty. The huge birthmark on Alai's face distinguished him from his twin, Haidar. Drafted at the beginning of the war, neither had been anxious for soldiering, but resisters were hanged. Home was a Moslem village near Hadjin, but religion meant nothing to them. Their only purpose was to satisfy themselves, and the war had disrupted their self-indulgent ways.

"Armenians are no better than hares and snakes," Alai said as he and his brother rode side by side. He hated the Young Turks' idea of equality for Christians and recalled the battle against Hadjin six years earlier. He was only thirteen then. His father had smuggled a wagonload of Martini rifles into town and had given them to his agitated Moslem friends. Alai and his brother each took a rifle and followed their father into the hills. He raised his head and sniffed, remembering the smell of sweet powder after firing. The rifle had given him an exhilarating feeling of power.

"I want to go home," Haidar said.

"*Sikdir*," Alai swore. "I miss our coffeehouse. Especially at night. I want to hear the music and dance. That's the life I want!" He was bored and ready for mischief. So was his brother.

"*Djehennem.* I'd give a month's pay for a drink of raki." Haidar pulled a canteen from his saddlebag and took a long swig of water. "Why don't we just ride away?"

"Ha, my funny brother. That's exactly what that damn Captain would like us to do. He'd love to use his whip on us." Alai spit. "*Djehenneme gedsin* to you captain!" Alai hated Khourshid. Reminded him too much of his own hard-nosed father, and he feared both men. One day he'd show them, he promised himself. "Haidar, those two girls are back there, nowhere near their father."

Haidar's narrow dark eyes sparked. He eyed the nearby wooded rolling hills. "Yes, yes, I see them. They are alone and on that good-for-nothing horse." Haidar jammed his heels into his horse as if he were meeting the enemy head on. Alai raced after him and saw Flora jump off the horse, running and screaming.

Haidar dismounted, caught her and tried to lift her onto his horse. He felt her nails scratch his arms and then her teeth pierced through his skin. He whacked her on the back of her head, and she went limp. Thrusting her up onto his horse, he remounted and pressed himself against her buttocks, kicked his horse and sped away.

In the meantime Alai went after Verkin, who sat paralyzed on the mare. Suddenly Grandmother Shushan appeared and maneuvered her donkey in front of him. He slapped her so hard she fell to the ground with a thud. Snatching the mare's reins, Alai galloped off into the woods in a cloud of red dust.

Hagop heard Flora's scream. He turned to see the soldiers riding off with his girls. "Captain!" he yelled. "Help me!" Levon sprinted ahead of his father, waving his hands high above his head. "Your men are taking my sisters!" he shouted, pointing to the woods. The billowing dust had not yet settled.

Khourshid kicked his horse toward the woods. He saw freshly etched tracks in the soft dirt road, raised his pistol and fired a shot in the air. The sound reverberated, bouncing off the rolling hills.

Alai heard the echoing sounds and reined in his horse. "*Sikdir*! It's the captain!" His face paled.

"Say they wanted to come," Haidar said.

"Stupid! Do they look as if they want to be with us?"

"Offer him one," Haidar said.

"Hmmm. Haidar, get off your horse!"

The brothers stood at attention and waited.

A livid Khourshid came to a sudden halt and shouted, "I could shoot both of you for this." He dismounted, helped Flora slip off Haidar's horse and lifted her onto the mare behind her sister. He slapped the mare and watched the horse take the girls away. He reached for his whip and walked toward the two soldiers, raising the whip up and down, "If either of you steps out of line again…" He circled the two soldiers and without warning snapped the whip toward Alai, barely missing his ear. Then he cracked it against Alai's legs, raised it and whipped it against Haidar's legs. "If you try this again you'll taste more than a whip. I'll see that both of you will swing at the end of a rope. Do you understand!"

"Yes, sir," Alai answered, his legs buckling.

Haidar, trying to stay steady, echoed, "Yes, sir."

"Then get on with your duties and don't dare touch any of the girls!" Khourshid tilted his head, hesitated, and swallowed the saliva forming in his mouth. He shouted, "You are a disgrace to the Turkish army!" He kicked his horse and rode away. Minutes later he saw the distraught family. Terror was still written on the faces of the girls, their mother was hysterical, and their grandmother sat by the side of the road, dazed. He dismounted. "Will your mother be able to continue?" he asked Hagop.

"She's bruised, but no bones are broken."

"Mrs. Munushian, let me help." Khourshid extended his hand, but Shushan turned away. He felt bad she wouldn't let him help her and noticed that the girls and their mother had rushed away.

"Mr. Munushian, you won't be bothered again, but it would be wise to keep your girls close to you at all times." Wanting to apologize, he said, "The Memoush Oghlou brothers are not good military material." He waited for a response that never came. "Most of our Moslem soldiers wouldn't abuse a woman," the captain continued. "I hope you won't hold this coarse incident against us."

Hagop still said nothing.

Khourshid understood. The hatred between the Armenians and the Turks had intensified since the deportation order. But he would do his best to minimize the suffering of those under his charge.

"Call upon me whenever you need help, Mr. Munushian." He remounted his horse and sped away. Trying to understand why he felt so protective toward these Armenians he let his mind drift back six years when he first came to Hadjin. The year was 1909, one year after the Young Turk's had stripped Sultan Abdul Hamid of his power. That's when the crafty old sultan attempted a coup. After 33 years as Sultan of the Ottoman Empire, Abdul Hamid didn't relinquish power easily and incited a Holy War, putting the country on the brink of civil war. Khourshid remembered riding through Hadjin's mountains sending home the angry armed Turks who were attacking the Armenians. "We have a new Sultan," he and his soldiers shouted to the militants hovering behind the hills. "Go home. Go home." He was a lieutenant then and felt lucky he'd been sent to Hadjin. Some of his fellow officers in Constantinople had been murdered by their own enlisted men.

Maybe that's why he felt the way he did. The Hadjin assignment may have saved his life.

CHAPTER EIGHT

RESIGNATION

Billowy clouds were forming. In the distance a streak of lightning flashed, then thunder cracked. Grandmother Shushan looked up into the darkening sky. Wind whipped against her face. Drops of rain started to fall. Was this an omen?

"Come, Mother," Hagop said as people scattered to find refuge. Trying to lift her, his legs buckled. He motioned for his son. "Levon, help me."

Levon rushed over and picked up his grandmother. With his father by his side they moved haltingly toward a small grove of sycamore trees. Overhead two more bursts of thunder crashed. A deluge of rain drenched them before they reached the grove. Levon gently lowered his frail grandmother onto the damp ground, rested her against the trunk of a tree, and gently brushed his hand over her wet face.

Shushan breathed a sigh of relief. She was grateful to still be alive, but for how much longer? She closed her eyes wanting to bury the day's tragedy into a dark oblivion of sleep, but the rain seeping through the branches and dripping on her kept her awake. She was so tired, she just wanted to sleep, maybe even forever. Suddenly a vision flashed in front of her eyes. It faded quickly. She had seen it before... on the first night of the march... *thousands and thousands of Armenians stilled in the desert sands under a burning hot sun.* Shaken, more images began to appear...her childhood, her parents, her children, and her late husband, Ruben. Her strength was going. She could feel it. She had lived a long life and no longer feared death, but she didn't want to be left behind to die alone by the side of a road. Would they, *could* they leave her?

She heard a faint voice in her head calling, *Shushan... Shushan.* It sounded like Ruben.

CHAPTER NINE

A DREADFUL NIGHT

Wet and shaken, Flora curled up into a ball, as if she was back in the womb. She had been so close to being kidnapped, raped, and who knows what else? Quaking all over, she tried to control her trembling arms by gripping her fists hard. She and her sister were nothing but toys in the hands of those soldiers, who could have thrown them away, into any old ditch, whenever they tired of playing with her or Verkin.

That face! Startled, she bolted to a sitting position. He was the soldier in that frightening dream where she was falling and falling with no end in sight. It was at the American College in Constantinople and she remembered waking up that morning in a cold sweat, plagued by the dream.

The one who tried to abduct her, he was the soldier in the dream who had pushed her off the cliff. Why would she dream of him, *before she even knew him?* She tried to piece together those days, one year ago, at the college in Constantinople. And then she remembered. Flora and her friends, Ana and Sona, had been invited to accompany Dr. Patrick, the lady president of the college, and Miss Webb to attend a reception at the American Embassy in Constantinople. The embassy's ballroom was the most magnificent room she had ever seen. Smartly dressed waiters in white jackets served the guests. She had never before seen men, let alone elegantly dressed men, serving food. And then one approached and offered her *baklava.* She remembered trying to hide her shock when she first saw his pockmarked face and squirming as he continually rubbed the back of his hand with his thumb. He asked her if he could visit her at the college when Miss Webb rescued her, warning her never to talk to strange men. Then he showed up at the college the next day looking for her. Dr. Patrick and Miss Webb got upset and went into great detail, telling her about an American girl who had disappeared. They feared that the girl had been kidnapped by white slavers and warned Flora to be careful. Flora had never before heard of the white slave trade, and Miss Webb feared the waiter could have been part of that gang.

"Yanko," Flora said aloud. "His name was Yanko." *Was the dream a warning? Is there some sort of...something?...with Yanko and the soldier?* Wanting to hide all of her, her body and her wounded soul, she drew her knees to her chest and dropped her head deep into her arms, but the tremors in her arms were a reminder of her reality. Finally, she fell into a fitful sleep.

She awoke with a start. It was morning. The rain had stopped. But she was drenched. Drops of rain clinging on the leaves began to drip on her head. She frantically searched the grove for her parents and saw them sitting together under a sycamore tree, her mother stroking Avedis's wet hair as he leaned against her. Dickran had snuggled up against Hagop. God forbid, she didn't want to lose them. Reaching for Miss Webb's Bible, she held it close to her heart. "Please, God, let me be strong!" Tears streamed down her cheeks. Her parents were losing their vitality, her loving grandmother was seriously ill, her education had been taken away, her hopes and dreams were fading, and yesterday she and her sister were nearly...*who knows how awful it could have been*! "Oh God, if you really exist, please help us." Then she saw Verkin sitting in the wet field away from the rest of the family and thought it peculiar. Especially after yesterday. "Verkin?" she called out and slowly approached. "Verkin?"

Not answering, Verkin sat rigid, drawing a square in the wet grass with a stick. She drew the square over and over and then lunged at it slashing it with X's.

Flora gently placed her hand on her shoulder.

"No!" Verkin yelled.

"It's me, Flora!" she exclaimed, jumping back after noticing Verkin's strange eyes. They looked empty. She reached out and pulled Verkin to her saying, "We'll be all right. Father won't let anything happen to us. We'll be all right," she repeated over and over, only to see that Verkin still had that odd look in her eyes.

What can I do to pull her out of this? Flora asked herself. Not understanding where her strength was coming from, she grasped her sister's hand. "Verkin, help me find some mint for tea." Together they drifted through the wet grass and found a batch of wild mint. Flora carefully picked the mint, gave the long stems to Verkin, and Verkin methodically turned them into a bountiful bouquet. They walked back to the grove, Verkin following Flora almost as if she were guided by something other than her own consciousness.

"Good," Hagop said, taking the mint, not noticing Verkin's strangeness. He touched his mother's forehead. "Grandmother's very hot. And Nubar has been coughing. Tea could help." He glanced toward the road. Who is that riding this way?"

"It's the captain," Flora said.

Moments later the rider came to a halt in front of Hagop. "Mr. Munushian, I've assigned the Memoush Oghlou brothers to the head of the convoy," Captain Khourshid said. "That way I'll know where they are at all times."

Hagop knew the captain was saying those soldiers wouldn't be anywhere near his daughters. "Thank you," he managed to say.

"How is your mother this morning?"

"Very ill."

"Can she travel?"

"I dare not leave her behind."

"You and your family can rest here and join the next convoy if you like."

"No. We'll continue." Hagop felt safe with Khourshid.

"Mr. Munushian, I have something to help your mother." Khourshid reached into his saddlebag and gave Hagop six white pills.

Before Hagop had a chance to say thank you, the captain rode away. Hagop wished he had told Khourshid how grateful he was, even though the man was a Turk. He looked at the pills in the palm of his hand and put one into his mother's mouth. The boys had already gathered their belongings. Everything was wet, including the one remaining sack of flour. "Bring the donkey," Hagop yelled to Toros.

Levon hitched the cart to the mare, now emptied of all their food except for the one sack of wet flour. Hagop couldn't bring himself to throw it away, even though it was probably useless. He placed his mother into the cart, the two youngsters on one of the donkeys, and walked toward the muddy road.

Hunger pains stabbed at his stomach. There was no food, and he couldn't remember the last time he had eaten. Nubar was sick. His mother was feverish. What if she couldn't continue? Could he abandon her? Reaching for the money belt clinging to his body, he wondered what good was the gold he had hidden. There was no place to buy food. And even if there were, the Turks were reluctant to sell anything to Armenians. He gazed into the peaceful blue sky and wondered how a loving God could allow such suffering.

CHAPTER TEN

FAMILY LOVE

Worried for her sister, Flora walked arm in arm with Verkin. "We can't let those rotten soldiers poison our spirits," Flora said, trying to rekindle her own strength. "We can't let them rape our souls."

Verkin remained uncomfortably silent.

"Did I ever tell you the story Dr. Patrick told me about Sultan Murad and his daughters?" Flora asked hoping her incessant chatter would lift the darkness shadowing her sister.

Verkin's eyes began to soften. "All you ever talk about since you came home from Constantinople is Miss Webb this and Dr. Patrick that." Verkin hesitated, then, with a hint of normalcy, asked, "Who's Sultan Murad?"

"Sultan Abdul Hamid's older brother. Abdul Hamid said his older brother was crazy and locked him and his family in the basement of a palace. They didn't even have mattresses to sleep on."

"A palace with no beds?"

"Oh, it was a beautiful palace, but the basement was their prison. Murad's wife and one of his three daughters died, but Sultan Murad and his other two daughters never lost their spirit. There was nothing in that cold, damp room but scraps of wood and an old, discarded piano. That supposedly *crazy* man taught his daughters how to play, and one of the princesses was so talented she wrote a composition when she was only eight years old."

"Princesses?"

Flora nodded and felt refreshed as Verkin began to respond. "They suffered too," she said. "But, Sultan Murad was a remarkable man. He used charcoal they needed for fuel to teach his daughters to write on the scraps of wood. That's how he taught them to read. He even taught them Persian poetry from his memory. The princesses loved their father. Their bond was always strong, even after Abdul Hamid released the girls and forced them into marriages when they turned eighteen."

"Eighteen! They were locked up all those years?

"Uh huh. Sultan Murad was in that basement for 28 years. And then he was strangled."

"How come you never told me this story before?"

"I guess I didn't think about it before today. Now, I understand how much they suffered. It's funny," Flora said. "The princess, the one who wrote the piano compositions, told Dr. Patrick that when she got married and lived in a grand estate with more servants than she knew what to do with, had beautiful clothes, and a fine piano, she said she felt like a bird locked in a cage. She said she had more freedom when she was confined in that palace basement and living in rags."

"She wore rags?"

"Yes. They had only rough gray material for clothing, you know, the kind that's used in soldier's uniforms. It was one more way Abdul Hamid tried to break their spirits, but he couldn't, so strong was their love for one another."

Verkin tightened her arm against Flora's, their shoes squeaking in the wet, muddy road. Suddenly they stopped. Their father was agitated and cursing.

"Damn it!" Hagop swore.

The cart was stuck in the mud. It wouldn't budge, even as Levon and Toros pushed against it and their father and Nubar pulled at the mare's reins.

"We need planks, or something flat to slip under the wheels," Hagop yelled to Levon.

"Yes, Father." Levon reached into the cart, lifted Grandmother Shushan and gently placed her on dry ground by the edge of the stream. "Toros, come with me." They headed for the woods while Hagop and Nubar examined the sunken cart.

"Sit by the stream," Hagop called out to them.

Flora lifted Avedis from the donkey. "I want to go home," Avedis whimpered. "I'm so hungry." Flora pressed the scrawny youngster against her chest, rocking him and setting him down on the ground next to Grandmother Shushan. Verkin followed Flora, with her six year old brother, Dickran. Dickran sat beside Grandmother, nestling his little hips against her body. "I know a story, Grandmother. About a poor rich man."

Shushan brushed her hand through his wet hair. "Tell me," she said, drawing a whimpering Avedis closer.

Dickran gazed into his grandmother's warm, tired eyes. "*A long time ago there was and was not a rich man and he was very unhappy and the poorest man in the village was very, very happy....*

Watching Dickran trying to cheer up Grandmother Shushan, Flora said, "See, our love for one another is as strong as Sultan Murad's family."

Verkin took off her shoes, slipped her muddy feet into the stream, lifted her tattered skirt and poked her finger through the frayed holes. "I can't imagine a princess wearing rags."

Flora smiled and reminisced about the princess whose talent was never nurtured. Dr. Patrick had told Flora that one of the princess's compositions was played in Constantinople by a visiting Russian orchestra and the conductor was amazed the princess could write such a piece without formal training. Flora wondered if the princess hadn't been locked up all those years, would she have been allowed to develop her talent? But, then, she was still only a girl, even if she was a princess, and Turks didn't look upon girls the same way as they did boys.

"Your place is in the home." Flora sighed, remembering her father's words and wondering why men couldn't admit that girls had brains and talent too, just like boys. Her eyes scanned the muddy road full of innocent people trying to cope with the misery brought upon them by warring politicians. *What good had these men and their brains done for this world? They've brought us war, that's what they've done,* and she wondered what the world would be like if it were run by women like the princess, Dr. Patrick and Miss Webb.

Her thoughts were interrupted as Verkin asked, almost wistfully, "Will I ever wear a clean, pretty dress again?" Flora reached for her sister's hand and said, "You'd love the stylish dresses women in Constantinople wear. I hope one day you can see and touch the rich fabrics for yourself. I can picture you in one of those wonderful Paris fashions right now." Flora gently squeezed her sister's hand and said, "Verkin, if Father said you could go to school instead of having to get married, what would you like to study?"

"Study?" Verkin sounded perplexed.

"Think about what would be the most wonderful thing you could create."

"That's easy. A beautiful dress."

"Would you like to study with someone who could teach you how to design a dress?"

"I never thought about it. It would be nice." Verkin spread out her ragged skirt. "What would they tell me to do with this?"

"Throw it away," Flora said and burst into laughter. Putting her arm around Verkin, she said, "Let's really dream." She took a deep breath. "I see you in Paris, studying with the greatest dress designers in the world."

"Paris?"

"Yes! You and Levon together."

"Really? And what about you?" Verkin asked. "Would you like to go back to Constantinople?"

"Ohhh, Constantinople was wonderful, but I have bigger dreams." Flora threw her arms up in the air, reaching toward the heavens. "America!"

"You and Antranig! Me, I like the idea of going to Paris."

"There's a college in America that has something to do with the missionaries. Miss Webb said I should think about going there. I have a hard time remembering its name. I have to think of God, before the name comes to me. Yes. It's Holy, like a holy mountain. That's it! Mount Holyoke!"

"No!" Flora heard her father scream. Both girls turned to see their father's face had turned ashen. The cart they were pushing slammed into a boulder and broke a wheel in two.

Hagop became livid. "Levon, put Grandmother on Esh. The boys will ride the mare." He unhitched the cart. "Let's go!" He picked up a rock and heaved it at the wrecked cart.

"What about the flour?" Levon asked.

"Leave it!" Hagop said and started walking. "Leave the God damned thing in the broken down cart!"

Flora and Verkin put on their wet shoes, the soles now full of holes and followed the family. They walked side by side through the mud, not aware of their discomfort. Both were dreaming grand thoughts of what could be.

* * *

That night as Flora lay to sleep she had her nightly talk with Miss Webb. She told her teacher how scared she had been, for herself as well as for Verkin, how grateful she was that her sister was no longer mournful, and how happy she was that, for the first time, she felt a close bond with Verkin, like that of her mission friends, Ana and Sona, but felt bad it took such a horrific experience to bring them together.

CHAPTER ELEVEN

CLOSED IN

Two days later the convoy reached the Amanus mountains, in the village of Memoreh. Flora first noticed the field. A wire fence, like an animal enclosure, surrounded masses of Armenians packed inside. The message was clear. Even though no one had the freedom to leave the forced march, the fence suggested imprisonment, like ordinary convicts. Then she saw them and her heart skipped a beat. Sitting on horses waiting for the Hadjin convoy to file through the open wooden gates were the Memoush Oghlou brothers. A huge smile crossed Alai's face when he saw Verkin. "Father!" she called.

"I see them," he whispered. "Levon, stay close to the girls," Hagop said with a quiet urgency and watched Levon and Arpi hover over both girls. Then he placed himself and his donkey carrying Shushan between the girls and the soldiers as they passed through. Once inside, he looked back. Alai was still smiling, his eyes fixed on Verkin. Hagop's face paled.

Fear surged through Flora's body. Neither she nor her sister would be able to let down their guards. But as her family blended in and become anonymous within the field thick with refugees, relief flooded over her. She wondered if Ana and Sona were out there, somewhere. But everyone looked alike—ragged, dirty, matted hair, exhausted and realized it would be too painful to see her friends in these circumstances. Their hopeful sparks had been snuffed out, too. Then she realized she hadn't seen any young men.

* * *

Red poppies and widely scattered trees dotted the vast area, as if a bird had randomly dropped only a few seeds. Hagop kept walking, wanting to get away from the heavy stench permeating the area and his fellow Armenians, who had been reduced to a disheveled resemblance of humanity. Then he realized the field was filled with women, children and old men. He glanced at Levon and felt the knot in his stomach tighten.

Helping his mother off the donkey and settling her under the umbrella of a laurel tree, he felt her shivering. Shushan was hot, perspiring and her breathing labored. He helped her stretch out, trying to make her comfortable, and the family gathered around.

"How is she?" Arpi asked.

"Not good." Gently, Hagop rubbed his mother's forehead. He gazed into her eyes and saw a dull withdrawal. He feared she wouldn't survive the night. "We need water," he said.

"I'll get some." Levon picked up the water bag and rushed to a nearby stream.

"Mother needs food."

"We all need food," Arpi said softly and slumped down on the ground.

When Levon returned, Hagop put his arm beneath his mother's shoulders and dripped a little water on her lips. Lifting her head, he put the bag to her mouth.

Her eyes opened wide. "Ruben, is that you?" she wheezed through a whisper. She made a gurgling sound and slumped against Hagop's arm.

"Mother. Mother!" Hagop couldn't hold back his tears. "She's gone." He gently closed his mother's eyes. "Grandmother is gone."

"Gone?" Avedis asked.

"To heaven."

"No!" he cried and ran to Arpi, tears streaming down his dirty face.

Arpi picked him up and rocked him, saying between labored breaths, "I know, I know."

"We have to bury her," Hagop said.

"I know where," Levon said.

"I'll help," Nubar said.

"No. You rest." Hagop said. Nubar was getting weaker by the day, his frame wasting away.

Levon lifted Shushan's body. "The area is close by," he said and walked ahead of his father. "When I went to get water, I saw two shovels and wondered."

"Now you know," Hagop said. "Should we be grateful to the Turks for their consideration?"

Levon didn't answer.

They reached the area, and Hagop noticed several soft mounds of dirt. He held his breath. The pristine area was shadowed by death. He picked up a shovel, and he and his son dug the grave in silence. A dull thud, the sound of dirt hitting his mother's body, rang in his ears.

It was a sound he would never forget.

CHAPTER TWELVE

A COMPASSIONATE MAN

Captain Khourshid was seated in an overstuffed chair in the common room of the officer's barracks, his feet resting on a frayed leather ottoman. His stomach was full, his first hot meal in two weeks, and he was relaxed and comfortable. He slowly passed a cigar under his nose, savoring the smell of the fine Turkish tobacco. He moistened the cigar with his mouth, bit and spit away its tip and struck a match on the bottom of his boot to light it. He took a long drag, blew out a series of smoke rings and watched them spiral toward the ceiling. *Pleasure, pure pleasure,* he thought. He was smiling, something he had not done a lot of lately.

On the floor next to his chair was a crumpled newspaper. He picked it up, smoothed out the front page of one of Constantinople's popular papers, the *Ikdam*. "ANOTHER ENGLISH SHIP SUNK," the headline screamed. He glanced at the date. The paper was three weeks old.

Gallipoli. That's where the action was. That's where he wanted to be. He'd had enough of this convoy duty. After all, he was a professional soldier and good soldiers were needed at the front to keep the English from encroaching on his beloved country.

He detested leading the Hadjin convoy. It was punishment for expressing his shock at the extent of the Armenian directive. *"We are not barbarians,"* he had said. Now he was paying the price of his candor. "If you care about the Armenians so much, maybe you should go with them," his commanding officer had said and handed him the orders. That was the last time Khourshid let his personal scruples rule his good sense in front of his superiors. He thought the deportation order unworthy of a great and civilized empire. He liked to think he still had a trace of humanity left in him.

The door opened, and a Turkish officer entered. The man saluted, clicked his heels, bowed slightly and said, "Captain Rafael de Nogales."

Khoushed rose from his chair and returned a casual salute. "Khourshid," he said, wondering why his precious leisure was being interrupted.

"Pleased to meet you," de Nogales said in Turkish with a heavy accent.

"Where are you from?"

De Nogales smiled. "Venezuela."

Khourshid scanned the Venezuelan from head to toe. He'd heard about this soldier of fortune.

"Colonel Aghia asked me to deliver this telegram to you."

"The man the soldiers call the Lord and Master of Mount Amanus?" Khourshid asked and laughed.

"The very same," de Nogales answered, his manner cold.

Wondering if the man feared the Colonel, Khourshid quickly changed the subject. "Are you relieving me of my convoy duty?"

"No," he replied. "I'm in charge of supplying ammunition to our troops in Palestine so they can take the Suez. At the moment I am simply the bearer of news." He handed Khourshid the telegram. "It appears the powers in Constantinople have plans for you."

Khourshid tore open the envelope.

"REPORT IMMEDIATELY TO CONSTANTINOPLE. LEAVE TWO SOLDIERS BEHIND."

"Two soldiers?"

"Yes."

"Will they be under your command?"

"No. Colonel Aghia's."

Khourshid frowned. "I have good soldiers and some who are not."

"Good soldiers are needed at the front. The Colonel said to leave your two most expendable."

"Those are the Memoush Oghlou brothers," he said.

"I don't care what their names are. Just tell them to report to Colonel Aghia in the morning." De Nogales said no more and clicked his heels.

Khourshid watched him go. The Colonel's order was strange, but he didn't think beyond that. Happy to be rid of the Memoush Oghlous, he sat back in the comfortable chair and finished his cigar.

The next day Khourshid led his small band of soldiers away from the camp. They had to pass along the edges of the crowded field. He wanted get clear of the place, but he couldn't help glancing over at the gray mass of exhausted bodies and wondering about the Munushian family. In a way he was relieved that he didn't see them. There was little more he could have done for them. Still he didn't like the vague feeling of guilt that churned in his stomach.

The stench of human waste and misery was overpowering. He kicked his horse into gallop, but couldn't get away from the sight of the wretched. Just beyond the railroad station the road was blocked by another long column of ragged deportees. They were being herded toward the field. Khourshid's eyes fell upon a woman bent with age and sorrow. Her eyes were pleading.

"Sir, have you bread?"

He turned his head away, but another sight awaited him, a child— he couldn't tell its sex—who was holding the hand of a blind man. The man stood tall, a great white beard flowing over his naked chest. His face had something noble in it, maybe nothing more than resignation. His sightless eyes were directed upward in search of a blessing that never came.

Overpowered with more emotion, Khourshid jammed his heels into his horse and sped away. He couldn't erase the picture of the blind man from his mind. But there was no way he could escape the tragic scenes. As far as he could see long lines of Armenians were struggling. He saw no break in the columns for five miles. Stragglers had collapsed. Men digging graves glared at him, their eyes filled with hatred. He didn't want to be a recipient of that hatred. It was his superiors who said Armenians were traitors and *all* had to be punished. He just wanted to be in Gallipoli, where a soldier could fulfill a real duty to his country, an honorable one.

Then he witnessed something strange. Ten convicts chained together and under the guard of an armed soldier on horseback walked in the middle of the road. Khourshid assumed they were on their way to Memoreh to join the labor battalions extending the railroad onto Baghdad.

But he was wrong.

CHAPTER THIRTEEN

AN OPPORTUNITY

The Memoush Oghlou brothers entered the smoke filled room, and Alai felt his knees wobble. The commanding officer, Colonel Aghia, looked mean and agitated as he rustled through a stack of papers on his desk.

Pushing the papers aside, Aghia cursed, lifted his dark eyes and fastened them on the two soldiers. "Two of a kind!" he bellowed and couldn't hold back a raucous laugh. Still laughing, the colonel settled back into his chair. Regaining his composure, he said, "Captain Khourshid is leaving you under my command. He has been ordered to Gallipoli."

Alai wanted to jump for joy. He was free from Khourshid!

"The road through the mountain pass is perilous and must be widened to accommodate the safety our supply lines," the colonel said as if he were reading a statement from a fact-finding mission. "But the Armenians are being moved along the road everyday, and I don't want them impeding the progress of the labor battalions." He picked up a lit cigarette in the ashtray and smoked the rest of it never taking his menacing eyes off the two soldiers. Crushing it in an ashtray already full of butts, he flicked the butts toward a wastebasket, half of them landing on the floor. Taking another cigarette, he placed it in his mouth, stood tall and walked toward the two young soldiers. He struck a match on the bottom of his boot, lighted the cigarette and inhaled the first puff deeply. He curled his lips and blew the smoke directly into Alai's face.

Alai didn't dare move.

"I'm assigning you the task of taking the Armenians in camp to Aleppo."

Alai couldn't believe what he just heard. Did the colonel mean that he and Haidar were to be in command?

The colonel sauntered back to his desk and sat in the aged, wooden chair. It creaked. "Our Minister of Interior, Talaat Pasha, has released all Turkish prisoners so they can help our great empire win this war. Some arrived last evening. Four will assist you in completing your mission. They are now classified as gendarmes, will carry cudgels, but no guns."

Alai couldn't restrain the smile crossing his face.

"You'd better understand the importance of your responsibility!" the colonel said raising his body and voice with synchronizing tension. "And move those damn Armenians through the pass quickly!" He slammed his heavy fist against the desktop, sat back and his quick to anger facial expression rapidly changed into one of a scary mellow calm. "The convicts may consider deserting. Remember, headquarters knows who and how many are under your command." A half smile began to shape the lower part of his mouth. "If one of them does not reach Aleppo, I have given orders that both of you should be hanged."

Blood drained out of Alai's face. His brother swayed and Alai was afraid Haidar was going to faint.

"I see you understand your assignment," Aghia said and flashed his tormenting smile again. "I've told the convicts that any deserter will be shot, whether Armenian or Turk!" He paused. "You *will* shoot them, if they try to escape." He opened the desk's drawer, pulled out a revolver and pointed it at Haidar and then to Alai. "Understand!"

"Yes, Sir!" the two soldiers responded in unison. Alai could feel drops of urine sliding down his leg. He stood rigid, as if frozen, trying not to wet his pants.

The colonel slipped the gun into the holster strapped around his waist. "Wait outside for further orders," he said, as if he wanted to be rid of them.

Alai wasn't sure his legs would carry him out. His brother's face was ashen. When they reached the corridor and heard the door close behind them Alai began to sweat profusely.

If he had to shoot one or all of the convicts, how could he convince headquarters that not even one had deserted or escaped?

CHAPTER FOURTEEN

A DANGEROUS TURN

The morning was bright and sunny, but Flora felt as if black clouds were about to pour havoc on them. Death was in the atmosphere. She felt it with the loss of Grandmother Shushan. Dying in this terrible place had a significance she didn't want to face. Who'd be next? Her eyes fell on Nubar. She knew it would be he. She gazed at her mother. Once robust, Arpi's ragged dress hung over a bony frame, her flesh melting away with each passing day. Her father was still a tower of strength, but his face was becoming drawn and haggard.

Avedis whined continually, but her six-year-old brother, Dickran, was the one who amazed her. The youngster had acted with such compassion toward his grandmother that she began to think of her six-year old brother as a grown-up in a little body.

She felt a closer bond with Verkin than she ever had and was sorry she hadn't shared great dreams with her sister before now. Having felt that her sister was filled with vanity, Flora realized that she was the one who was totally self-absorbed. But here, walking on this road for weeks on end to someplace, *to nowhere*, what difference did it make? When she was surrounded with important people in Constantinople, Flora convinced herself she was pretty special. She loved the huge cosmopolitan city and so did her friends, Ana and Sona. She wished she could find them. Should she look for them again? No, she decided. She didn't want to see them in these horrid circumstances.

How long had they been on the road? She didn't know for sure. Time no longer had meaning.

Hearing horses, she turned to see eight soldiers and four gendarmes. The Memoush Oghlou brothers were among them, but not Captain Khourshid. She ran to her father and grasped his hand. An officer stopped at the camp's entrance. An uncertain silence permeated the crowd. People cautiously rose to their feet.

Hagop turned to Levon. "Quickly, load everything onto the donkeys."

Four of the soldiers rode into the camp. An officer shouted "Males between the ages of 14 and 45 report to me, now!"

People panicked. Mothers threw dresses on their young sons. Men bolted. A soldier raced after the fleeing men and fired a shot. A boy fell to the ground, and the others stopped in their tracks. The soldier swung his cocked rifle toward the gate. "Move!"

Hagop's face paled.

Flora watched another soldier turn in her direction. He took the reins of the mare and pointed his rifle at Levon. "Move!"

"No! Don't go!" Avedis ran toward Levon.

Flora yanked her little brother back.

Arpi was frantic. "No! Levon," she cried out "Levon. My Levon."

Hagop braced Levon against his chest, hugging him, not wanting to let go. Levon pulled away and followed the trail of young men being forced away. He did not look back.

Hysterical women were running after their men pleading for them not to leave. Some hung onto them, but the soldiers pushed them away. Marching away from camp the young Armenian men turned for a last glimpse of their loved ones.

Flora searched the long line for Levon. She couldn't find him. Tears streamed down her face. Would she ever see him again?

"Flora," her father called. His eyes wet, he pointed to the donkeys. "We'd better get ready."

Flora helped Toros load their possessions and felt the intensity of the uncontrollable emotion in the air. Women were numb. Many did not have animals to carry heavy items. What to take? Clothing? Blankets? Tents? A pot to cook with? Indecision was on their faces.

She searched the area for the twin soldiers and saw them sitting on their horses, watching and waiting. Four gendarmes, cudgels strapped to their waists, stood near the gate. They did not look like men of charity, and women covered their faces as they left the camp. No one said they were to leave, but everyone knew they were to be herded away from their protective men.

"There are still several hundred of us," Hagop said. "Merge into the middle. We don't want to stand out." He kept his eyes on the twin soldiers. "Arpi, give Verkin your shawl. Flora cover your face with grandmother's *charshaf!*"

Taking the black kerchief, Flora wrapped it loosely around her head and face. She could smell her grandmother's scent. Tears welled, but she kept her focus on Alai who sat on his horse by the gate. She watched Haidar moving people against the edge of the road and into a single line. Her fear surged. Would they recognize her?

Keeping her head down as she passed through the gate, she felt relieved as she and her family easily passed by the gendarmes and the two soldiers. Filing into the single line and keeping her focus on the ground, she heard her father say, "I'm just behind you. Stay close together."

Shortly after, a cavalry unit came into sight. "More soldiers," Flora said to her father. Belts of ammunition strapped around their bodies and rifles cinched to their backs, the Turks kicked up dust as they rode by.

Levon. Flora couldn't bear the thought that he might be killed. Anger surged through her body. She picked up a rock, raised her arm ready to throw it and felt her father snatch it from her hand.

"Don't be foolish. I dare not think what he would do if you hit him."

Flora nodded, realizing she could have put her whole family in danger.

* * *

Hours passed. No time to rest. The gendarmes forced everyone on, not even allowing mothers stay with children who couldn't keep up. But no one in her family complained, not even Nubar. Sick as he was, he kept going, following in her father's tracks. Her admiration for him grew by the hour.

Finally, when the sun was low, they were allowed to rest for the night. Some fell by the side of the road too tired to find a more comfortable space. Sobbing, a filthy little boy, no more than three was crying, "Mother! Where's my mother?"

"I'll help you find your mother." Flora tried to pick him up, but didn't have the strength.

I'm so hungry," he cried.

"I'll take him," Nubar said. "Don't leave your father's sight." He picked up the child, coughing and stumbling as he searched for the child's mother.

Flora wondered how long Nubar could continue to push his failing body.

* * *

In the middle of the night, the donkeys shifted nervously in the moonlight. Hagop woke, blinked and sat up. He heard a girl scream, then the night was quiet again. His eyes met his wife's. "The girls. They'd better sleep with us." Glancing at his daughters, he nodded. Flora and Verkin slipped in between their mother and father. They lay so close their bodies touched. They didn't dare sleep.

* * *

Worrying that the convict-gendarmes would try to escape, Alai came up with a plan. He would offer the convicts a fresh girl every night. He and his brother, with rifles ready, would accompany them away from the convoy and watch as each lined up to take his turn. Then after he and his brother satisfied themselves, he'd let the gendarmes go at it again.

The plan worked that first night. But Alai wasn't taking any chances. He and his brother took turns sleeping, but Alai was fidgety all night long. The night before he had dreamt of two scaffolds, side by side. A knotted rope hung around his neck and the wood beneath his feet was ready to drop.

CHAPTER FIFTEEN

A QUAGMIRE

Dawn broke the next morning with a gentle pink hue spreading across the blue sky. The day should have been glorious and wonderful in the high valley, but in a meadow in the Amanus Mountains there was no joy, only hundreds of Armenians waking to another miserable day.

Verkin opened her eyes, sat up and saw a rare flower among a group of common daisies. Its face was covered with delicate white lace-like strands resembling a veil. The Turks called the flower the Bride's Head. Her eyes welled. Would she ever be a bride? Where had the Turks sent Armen? Would she see him again? Suddenly, she heard loud shouting.

"Up!" gendarmes shouted. "Up!" Poking their cudgels at sleeping bodies they yelled, "Get up and move!"

"The donkeys! They're gone!" Nubar screamed, looking toward the heavy rock where he had tied both donkeys the night before.

Hagop hastily scanned the area. The animals and everything on them were gone. His face paled. "Pick up what's left. Hurry!" He was going to miss those donkeys. Now the two young ones would have to walk the whole way. "Toros, stay with me." He picked up Avedis. "Arpi, mix in with everyone else, but keep Dickran with you. Flora, you and Verkin stay with Nubar." Flora hurled the water bag onto her back and clutching her Bible, she followed Nubar who had already merged into the long line of Armenians trudging up the dirt road.

Infantry soldiers heading to Palestine passed by throughout the morning. More soldiers followed packs of donkeys and mules carrying supplies. Hagop felt safer with so many soldiers marching alongside. His family wouldn't be obvious.

The day was getting warmer. Sounds of gurgling water followed the convoy. Hagop crossed the road to the stream. His arms ached from carrying Avedis for the last three hours. Setting his son down, he slipped off the extra shirt he had slept in to keep warm. Slowly the rest of the family joined them. No one talked. They simply drank from the stream. Hagop took the water bag from Flora and filled it. There was no food. He couldn't remember when he last ate. His ribs were protruding.

"Can you walk awhile?" he asked his small son.

Avedis nodded, his eyelids heavy. He had been quiet and lethargic all morning.

"Try to stay together," Hagop said, looking at the line of Armenians extending ad infinitum, with no end in sight. His eyes searched for the Memoush Oghlou brothers and not seeing them, he felt relieved. "If we get separated I'll find you at rest time." He looked up into the sky. "Probably in about two hours." Then the sun would be directly overhead "Come, Avedis." Hagop stretched his hand toward his young son, and they walked together for only a short distance. The road became steeper, and Hagop lifted Avedis onto his back, Avedis draping his arms around his father's neck. The steepest part of the incline was becoming toilsome, and Hagop forced one foot in front of the other. Alongside him was Toros, and Hagop commended his eleven-year old for keeping up.

By the time they neared the 7,000 foot summit, Hagop was exhausted. Hundreds were already scattered around the plateau at the top of the pass. Many were sitting with their backs against wind-bent pine trees that leaned just above the ground.

Soldiers were prodding a group of donkeys, and Hagop thought he saw Esh. Walking toward the donkey, he stopped, not daring to get too close. Some Turk might think he was trying to steal the animal and shoot him. Then, he saw Arpi. Her gait was strange. Why wasn't Dickran with her?

"Toros, watch your little brother. I'm going to help Mother." As he hurried down the road, he kept his eyes fixed on his wife. "Arpi?" He stood in front of her, his hands stretched toward her.

She stared through him.

"Arpi?" He took her hands in his. "Where's Dickran?"

"Dickran?" Her eyes were distant, as if she was not there.

My God, am I losing her? Squeezing her hands tightly, Hagop yanked them hard. "Dickran, where's Dickran!"

Her head jolted, as if an electric jolt passed through her body. "With Flora, I think."

His first impulse was to run down the road to find his six-year-old son, but he was reluctant to leave Arpi. He took her hand and led her the rest of the way. "Toros, give your Mother lots of water. I'm going to find Dickran." Rushing back down the road, he saw a familiar face. The wife of the man who owned the Hadjin rug factory limped along as she carried her two-year-son. Like the rest of the vital men in the convoy, her husband had been taken away.

"Have you seen my children?" he asked.

"With Nubar."

"Dickran too?"

She nodded, looking as if she were about to collapse.

"Let me help you." Hagop took the young boy and slipped his other arm around the gaunt woman. Before the deportation order this woman was lovely and lived in an attractive home. Now she was haggard and homeless. *It doesn't matter how educated or wealthy you are*, Hagop thought. *If you're Armenian, you're doomed.*

When they reached the summit, Hagop settled the woman, picked up the water bag and rushed away. He breathed a sigh of relief when he saw the rest of his family. Dickran was with his sisters. Nubar was wobbling. The girls were holding him up. Nubar, like everyone else, needed food and a full day's rest, but that was not to be. He approached them slowly. "Rest here," Hagop said, lifting the water bag. He sprinkled water on Nubar's head and face. "Here, drink."

"We have to find something to eat," Flora said. "Maybe food will help him."

"Let me think." Hagop, too, was feeling weak. But so was everyone else. He was desperate to find food.

When Nubar was ready to walk again, he led them to the plateau, where they blended in with the rest of the emaciated refugees crowding the only flat space on the summit. Arpi still had that strange, foreign gaze, but at this moment finding food was vitally important. "Come, Flora," he said and pulled her away. They walked into the woods scrounging the earth trying to find something, anything edible, to eat.

Suddenly he stopped. He saw Haidar leaning against a boulder, a rifle in his hands. Two gendarmes were with him, sitting side by side on the boulder.

"Oh, my God!" Flora said. Her mission friends, Ana and Sona, were clinging to one another.

A lustful smile crossed the face of one of the gendarmes as he jumped off the boulder. He released two buttons on his pants and rocked his hips in rhythm.

Rage poured up into Hagop's nostrils. He wanted to run, attack and kill that Turk. Instead, he grasped Flora's hand.

They raced away in silence.

CHAPTER SIXTEEN

A GREAT UNDERSTANDING

Horrified and numb, Flora slumped beside her sister. She couldn't tell Verkin about what she had witnessed. *Oh, Miss Webb*, she thought, *you don't want to know what I just saw.* Seething with anger that her father was so powerless, she knew that damn soldier would have shot him dead if her father had tried to protect her friends. *Oh God*, she thought. What if they had killed him? She'd be at the mercy of those soldiers and the hateful gendarmes. Her body trembled. Then, she noticed her mother staring into space. "Mother?"

Arpi didn't respond.

"Let me help you." Flora reached for the water bag and held it in front of Arpi's mouth.

"Oh," Arpi said, taking the bag.

"Take a drink, Mother."

Arpi raised the bag and drank for a long time.

Flora gently pulled away the bag and glanced toward her father. He, too, looked worried. "Mother. Come with me." Flora helped Arpi to her feet. They walked toward a wind-blown pine whose skimpy branches brushed against the ground. Then she heard Alai's thunderous voice. "Let's go!" She peeked through the branches and saw him. Alai rode alongside a Turkish officer as they followed another mule and donkey pack. Alai dismounted and waited for the officer and the animals to start down the pass. Then Alai started his descent on foot, his horse following behind. She thought that odd.

"Move!" shouted a threatening voice. Haidar and two gendarmes were yanking and pulling women onto the road.

"Quickly," she heard her father say. "Up, Nubar." He pulled Nubar to his feet, giving him a gentle push. "Toros, stay with Nubar. Verkin, keep Dickran with you." He picked up Avedis, who was fast asleep. "Flora, you watch Mother."

"Stay behind me, Mother," Flora said as she started her trek down the steep and narrow pass. Glancing over the edge, her heart raced. Now she understood why Alai chose not to ride his horse. The switchbacks were treacherous. Broken oxcarts and carriages lay at the bottom of the canyon. Then as she turned into the next curve, the road vanished. Part of it had slid into the canyon. Terrified, she felt as if her head was spinning. She hugged the side of the mountain and walked sideways until she cleared the drop. "Be careful Mother," she said.

Arpi didn't respond.

Flora watched as her mother walked along the perilous stretch of road as if it were a simple hill back home in Hadjin. At the sight of the next switchback, her tension eased. The pass had widened, and she hurried to keep up with her father. Why hadn't he warned her of the precipice? Had the section of road just dropped as she reached it?

The long column of exiles walked dangerously close to the cliff, not to interfere with the work of the men in labor battalions digging, shoveling, and breaking rocks into gravel. Flora picked her way through the rocks cluttering the way. She sidestepped a laborer, and suddenly the dirt under her feet gave way. Gasping, she began to slide down the side of the mountain, and the Armenian laborer snatched her arm. He yanked her back onto the road and handed her to Hagop.

Trembling, Flora felt her father's arms encircle her waist as he pulled her closer to him.

"You saved my daughter's life," Hagop said.

The man picked up his shovel and mumbled, "She might be better off dead."

Flora saw fear in her father's eyes. "I'll be all right," she said, steadied herself and stepped in front of him to stay within his grasp. Bracing her feet with every step, her legs ached by the time she reached the bottom of the pass.

Shadows of night crept along the area as the ragged Armenians searched for a patch of ground on which to rest. Flora saw a group of forlorn children huddled together. No adults were close by. She wondered if they could be from the orphanage. If so, where were Ana and Sona? Following her father through the maze of people, she spotted them. Flora gasped as their eyes met. Both girls cupped their hands over their bruised faces and turned away.

Flora wanted to run to them, throw her arms around them, cry with them, and tell them that one day everything would be all right again. She wanted to tell them to keep thinking about that college in America, the one with the funny name that Miss Webb wanted all three to attend. But she knew it would be kinder to pass on by.

A smattering of tents dotted the congested area, and Flora longed for cover, to be hidden from her hideous overseers. Those damn gendarmes had abused Ana and Sona, just like the girls kidnapped into the white slave trade.

"Keep walking," she heard her father say. His eyes focused ahead, he was canvassing the area, looking for comfortable space for the family. He must not have seen the two bruised girls, and she wasn't going to tell him.

The smell of sickness was everywhere. Dysentery affected every family. Nubar had it and was losing blood. Flora watched two Armenian laborers pick up a body and carry it across the narrow field. They threw it on top of corpses already piled in a wagon. Sorrow and anguish flooded over her father's face. She knew what he was thinking—that wagon represented the death of Armenia and all her people.

Flora wanted to run far away. Full of fury, she asked herself, *How could a loving and compassionate God allow this suffering. Why would God create a universe and have us suffer to such an extreme?* She knew what Miss Webb would say. *"When you suffer, so does God, just like parents suffer when their children go astray."*

Her mind was racing. Why do the Turks hate us? She asked herself if Mohammed and Christ met face to face, would they hate one another. Flora knew what Miss Webb would say… that true prophets would embrace, recognizing each other's deep love for God.

And she knew what her wise and loving Grandmother Shushan would say, *No, God doesn't create suffering. Man does.*

CHAPTER SEVENTEEN

A MALICIOUS MEETING

Sounds of horses neighing drifted from behind military housing. Soldiers on their way to Palestine were resting in the nearby village. Dust spiraled up from the dirt road as three soldiers rushed toward the local coffeehouse. The run-down shack whose white paint had grayed and was badly chipped was already crowded with soldiers sucking on water pipes and playing cards. Tobacco fumes hung in the air.

The four gendarmes with the Memoush Oghlou brothers were watching two soldiers playing backgammon. The one tossing his dice yelled *shesh besh* and threw his arm high in the air as the dice landed with a six and a five. A huge smile crossed the soldier's face.

At a nearby table Alai and Haidar puffed away on their first *nargile* in weeks. Stomachs full after a hot meal, the brothers felt somewhat relaxed from the stress of the last two days.

"This is more like it," Alai said and watched the water bubble as he sucked a long drag on the pipe. A look of contentment crossed his face.

The door opened and a pock-faced man in his early thirties entered and sat at a table next to the two young soldiers. Ordering *raki*, he smiled at Alai and took out a deck of cards. "Want to play?" He shuffled and three cards slipped off the table. Picking them up from the floor, he grinned, as if he was a novice.

"Why not?" Alai pulled a small coin from his pocket and slapped it on the table.

The pock-faced man nodded. "That's my kind of game." He carried his chair over to the young soldiers' table. "My name is Yanko." He sat down and placed his coin next to Alai's.

Alai won the first game easily. He twirled Yanko's coin with his fingers and pocketed it.

Yanko took another coin and slid it into the center of the table. "How about you?" he asked Haidar.

Snatching the cards, Alai said, "No! I feel lucky." He shuffled and quickly dealt.

Yanko smiled, exposing his stained teeth. He picked up his cards and played another sloppy game. "You win, again." Placing the palm of his hand over the back of his other hand, he rubbed it with his thumb. "If I'm not careful, you'll be taking all my money."

"I hope so," Alai said picking up the cards, anxious to play again.

"Maybe we can talk about some real money," Yanko said.

Alai flashed a curious smile. "What do you mean?"

"Girls. Can you get me girls?"

Alai and Haidar burst into laughter. "Sure. How many can you handle in one night?" Alai asked. He laughed, choked on saliva, coughed, and laughed again. The red color in his birthmark deepened.

Yanko waited for the young man to recover.

Haidar raised his brow, his eyes anxious. "How many, when, where and how much will you pay?"

"That depends."

"On what?" Alai said, wiping the corner of his eye as his laughter trailed off.

A soldier strumming his saz started to sing.

Yanko glanced at the soldier. "He's quite good."

Irritated, Alai looked over his shoulder to the singer. "Yes, he is." His head swung back toward Yanko. "Let's get back to what you really want."

Yanko pointed to a soldier dancing on the compacted dirt floor and said, "He's very good." A long pause. He turned to Alai. "Do you dance?"

"Yes, but I don't feel like it right now."

Becoming more anxious by the minute, Haidar asked again, "How much money are you talking about?"

Yanko smiled. "I don't want them for just one night."

Haidar frowned.

"How many nights?" Alai asked.

Yanko laughed. "Forever."

The brothers sat, momentarily stunned.

"Why?" Alai asked.

"That's my business, not yours."

"All right then. Just tell us how many and how much you'll pay," Haidar said.

"I want six girls and I'll pay a pound for each."

Alai swallowed. "Not enough."

Yanko ran his fingers through his hair. "All right. Two pounds each."

Haidar's breathing became noisy. "No. My uncle paid fifteen pounds for his wife."

Yanko leaned back. I don't want a wife or even care if they're virgins." Squinting, he asked, "How much does an officer make a month?"

"You mean if they get paid?" Alai asked. "We haven't seen any money since we left Hadjin."

"Hadjin?" Yanko asked. "You have girls from Hadjin?"

"That we do," Haidar responded, a smile spreading across his face.

"Hmmm. I once met a spunky girl from Hadjin. Yes, I'd like girls from Hadjin."

"We want five pounds for each girl," Alai stated with a firm voice.

"Five pounds! That's ridiculous." Yanko stood and took a step away from the table, as if he were going to leave. "There are other soldiers I can deal with."

"Not like us." Alai responded. "We are in command of the Hadjin convoy."

Surprised, Yanko reached for his chair and put his forefinger up to his mouth. He sat down and folded his arms on the table. "Officers are paid five pounds a month. I'm willing to give you three pounds for each girl. That's more money than your superiors make." Hesitating, he decided to say no more.

Alai turned to his brother. Haidar nodded. "It's a deal. When do you want them?"

"At sunrise. I want young girls, between the ages of fourteen and seventeen."

Alai reached into his pocket and pulled out a scrap of paper. He drew a map. "Meet us here."

Yanko folded the small piece of paper and carefully placed it in his shirt pocket. "At dawn I will pay you eighteen pounds for six girls." As he turned to leave, Yanko asked, "Are you on your way to Aleppo?"

"Yes," Alai responded.

"Maybe we can do business there too."

Alai glanced at the four gendarmes. Rubbing his neck, he thought about the noose that awaited him if any of the convict-gendarmes escaped.

Yanko waited. "You can find me at the covered bazaar in Aleppo."

A half-smile on his face, Alai nodded. He'd never let those damn convicts out of his sight.

"Go to the perfume stall near the doorway that leads into the square by the mosque and ask for Mahmud. He'll tell you where and when to meet me." Yanko nodded. "Sunrise."

Yanko walked outside and lit a French cigarette. He gazed at the peaceful, starlit sky. The threatening clouds of early evening had disappeared. He wished he could return to Constantinople. But that was impossible.

Lucky. Yes, he had been lucky to be the one who brought the last batch of girls to Aleppo. There he learned the whole gang in Constantinople had been arrested. He shuddered, thinking how he had resisted leaving the vibrant cosmopolitan city. But if he hadn't left, he, too, would be rotting away in a terrible Turkish prison. But, now, he saw an opportunity. With all the 'big shots' confined and shut away, he decided to take charge of the business. He knew the route. All he needed were procurers. The two soldiers? *Maybe.*

Walking behind the coffeehouse to his wagon, he climbed onto the buckboard and spread a bunch of hay into a comfortable mattress. Careful not to ignite the dry fodder, he sat on the edge of the wagon thinking about the two identical soldiers.

Damn fools, he sneered to himself, and the more he thought about how he set them up, the more he prided himself on knowing how to pick easy marks. It was only a matter of time. He'd see to it that they lost so much money they couldn't get out from under. But he'd have to be careful. His threats had to be believable. He didn't want them to disappear on him.

He flicked the cigarette toward a puddle, lay back and began his plan. *I have to know them better than they know themselves,* he thought.

Spineless. That was his reaction when he first spotted them. Yes they are, he nodded, as if agreeing with himself. Then his lips slid into a grin. *They're also cowards.* He'd seen plenty of brash, headstrong, asinine youngsters before. They strutted like peacocks fanning their manliness—as long as they held a loaded weapon. Take away the weapon, and they all cowered.

And he knew these two also liked to inflict pain. *Hmm,* he nodded. *I'll wager that their own pain thresholds are low... very low.* Could he keep them in line with the threat of *bastinado*? He'd make them believe his organization was so widespread that his men would find them *anywhere* in the empire and that the special treatment for debtors was bastinado. *Yes,* he nodded again. *That just might work.* He knew of more than one man who was driven mad from the intense pain of having the soles of his feet beaten with cudgels.

Yes, he'd think about that a bit more—after he observed the two soldiers... *a bit more.*

Tomorrow was crucial. Then he'd know if they were smart enough to deliver him many, many girls.

CHAPTER EIGHTEEN

ANOTHER FRIGHT

The next morning Flora awakened at dawn. For the first time in days, her stomach did not ache. Yesterday her father had canvassed the village and found a kind Turkish lady who had sold him bread. Sitting up, she eased away from her blanket, not wanting to wake those still sleeping. She crawled away.

"Where are you going?" Verkin asked.

Flora placed her finger against her mouth and whispered, "I'm going to give some of my bread to Ana and Sona." She tiptoed away and as she maneuvered around sleeping bodies, she saw a soldier and a man escorting six girls across the field. Why weren't the girls resisting? Two of them looked like Ana and Sona. Then the soldier turned. *Oh no!* Flora's heart sank and she fell to the ground. The birthmark on his face told her who he was. He and the other man lifted the girls into the back of a wagon. The pock-faced man climbed onto the buckboard, handed Alai something, and slapped the reins. The wagon trundled away.

The man on the wagon—he looked familiar. *Oh no!* She groaned. *The waiter from the embassy!* Helpless, she watched this terrible thing happening. Should she run to her father? What could he do? Her heart was beating furiously with fear and anger. Shaking, she watched Alai mount his horse and follow the wagon.

CHAPTER NINETEEN

A NEW FOUND PRIDE

Alai never before had so much money. The heavy gold coins in his pocket made a pleasurable sensation against his thigh. And there was so much more to come! He thought of home, but not with affection. He couldn't wait to throw his newly found money at his father's feet. That hard man with his threatening razor strap. The beatings. The unfairness.

Alai was the one who peed in his sleep in those days. Haidar never did. And he, not Haidar, was born with an ugly birthmark that covered half his face. Why him and not his brother?

"You will never amount to anything," his father yelled with each lash of the leather strap against Alai's buttocks. Remembering those beatings stoked the rage that simmered in Alai's gut. But, with fortune falling his way, he'd have more money than his father could earn in a lifetime. Now, he could demand respect from the hateful man. His only fond memory was the time the old man handed him the loaded rifle and said, "Go kill the Armenians in Hadjin." He still had that rifle—he loved it. People feared him when he carried it. He liked that feeling. And now, with gold in his pocket and more just waiting to come to him, his imagination ran wild. *Men will say, here comes Memoush Oghlou. Give him anything he wants and get out of his way.* He smiled and started thinking of his new accomplice. He slapped his thigh and rested his hand against the bulging coins, smiling, and anxious to gamble again. *I'm going to take Yanko for everything he's got.*

CHAPTER TWENTY

VULNERABLE ORPHANS

Flora struggled to regain her composure. Those stinking men were gone. Had they taken Ana and Sona? She started to shake. But maybe her friends were still here, after all. Reaching the area where she had seen them yesterday, she recognized a young girl from the orphanage. The youngster was crying.

"Where are Ana and Sona?' Flora asked her.

"They… went… with… the soldier," she said between choking sobs. "I wanted to go, too, but they wouldn't take me. They said Protestants didn't have to be exiled anymore, and they would take them to the Protestant minister in Aleppo." Sobbing, her nose running, she wiped her dirty hand under her nostrils. "I told them I was a Protestant too. I told them again and again, but they said I was too young. They should have taken me too," she cried.

"What's your name? How old are you?"

"Mary. I'm nine," she said, eyeing the bread.

Flora extended her hand, and the youngster snatched the bread and gulped it down.

"Flora!" She heard the anger in her father's voice as he rushed toward her. "You know I don't want you out of my sight!"

"Yes, Father. I'm sorry." And she meant it! She nearly blurted out that Ana and Sona had been taken away by a white slaver, but held back the words that wanted to spill out. There was nothing he could do.

Sleeping children stirred. Their eyes questioning, they slowly stood.

"Are they all from the Hadjin orphanage?" Flora asked Mary.

"Yes."

"There can't be more than twenty of you here. Where are all the others?" Flora asked.

"I don't know."

"The older orphans? Where are they?" Flora asked again.

"The soldiers took them away."

"Father," Flora said, "we have to help these children."

"We can barely help ourselves," he responded.

"But we can't leave them alone!"

"Noooo!"

Flora again said, "We can't leave them alone!"

Exasperated, Hagop threw his arms up in the air. The children walked toward him. The smallest one was no more than three years old, several looked no more than six, and none appeared to be more than ten. Their stringy hair was filthy and matted, making it hard to tell who was a girl or a boy. Three of the littlest ones didn't have shoes. They approached him and like newborn birds waiting to be fed, they stood in front of him, their pleading eyes fixed on him.

"All right," Hagop said. "But we have to organize the young ones."

Hagop looked at the young girl whose dirty face had a blotch of wet, runny mucus clinging to her cheek. "What's your name?"

"Mary." She was still sniffling.

Hagop took Mary's hand. "You and each of the older children are responsible for each of the younger ones. Never let them out of your sight. Do you understand?"

Mary nodded.

They paired each of the smaller ones with an older child, and Hagop instructed the scruffy group to stay together. He marched all twenty back to his family's campsite, wondering if he had completely lost his mind.

* * *

Noticing the children, Arpi's eyes widened. Verkin and Toros stopped folding the blankets and watched their father approach with the entourage of kids behind him. Nubar placed his hand on the ground, and he, too, slowly stood, watching.

"Are you the Pied Piper?" Arpi asked when Hagop arrived.

"No. Flora is."

"Mother," Flora said, "we couldn't leave them. They're orphans from the Hadjin mission."

"How are we going to feed them? And they're probably full of lice!"

Hagop returned Flora's smile. Arpi was her old self again.

Arpi scanned the scrawny youngsters. "Where are all the others? The older ones?"

Mary stepped forward. "They left. Protestants don't have to be exiled anymore."

"I don't understand." Arpi turned to Hagop. "The rumor about Protestants and Roman Catholics. That they can go home. Maybe it's true?"

"I doubt it," Hagop said. "I can only guess what has happened to the boys. More than likely, they were taken away, just like our Levon."

Pain crossed Arpi's face. "And the girls? Where are the older girls?"

"Some of them left with a soldier this morning," Mary said. She started to cry again. "They wouldn't take me. Said I was too young." She sniffled. "And I'm a good Protestant!"

"Ana and Sona?" Verkin asked. "Where are they?"

"With the soldier," Mary said, wiping her tears away.

"I saw six girls taken away this morning," Flora said. "They were put into a wagon."

"The gendarmes?" Hagop asked.

"No. Worse." Flora slumped to the ground.

"What do you mean?" Hagop knelt beside Flora. "What happened to them?"

"I think a white slaver took them away this morning."

Hagop placed his hand under Flora's chin and lifted her head. "How do you know about such things?"

"Miss Webb told me all about it in Constantinople. An American girl disappeared and Miss Webb thought the slavers took her."

"You're not telling me everything." Perspiration was beading on Hagop's forehead.

"I recognized the man who took them away. I saw him in Constantinople."

"My God, Flora! Are you sure?"

"He tried to be friendly, but Miss Webb wouldn't let him." The memory triggered a fluttering in her heart. Flora stood, trembling.

Arpi pulled her daughter to her chest, "I never should have let you go to Constantinople," she cried and embraced Flora with the little strength she had left.

Gendarmes were fast approaching, swinging cudgels over their heads.

"Hurry!" Hagop said, picking up Avedis. Turning to Flora and Verkin he said, "Be sure the children stay as close as possible. Tell them to look for us at rest time if they fall behind."

Hundreds converged onto the road. Others struggled to reach it. A young girl, about eight, pulled her sick mother to her feet. Taking the frail woman's hands, the girl walked backward pulling her mother toward the road.

Walk, walk, walk, till you drop is the Turkish way, Hagop thought. *There's no mercy for the frail, the sick, the old or the innocent.*

* * *

Soldiers filled the street. With ammunition and rifles strapped to their bodies, a folded cot attached to their saddle, they mounted their horses and rode off—on their way to war. Clogs of dirt kicked up, splashing against the weary Armenians sharing the road.

Nearing the street where the kind Turkish lady lived, Hagop realized he could sneak away to buy more bread. Gently placing Avedis on the ground, he said to his young son, "Stay with your mother." He touched his wife's shoulder. "We need more food. I'll find you later."

"No, Hagop. Don't go."

Glancing at the orphans, he said, "I have to."

His family watched as he disappeared behind the military housing. Flora rushed to her mother's side. "Where's he going?"

"To buy bread," she whispered and put her forefinger to her lips. "Go back to the children. Just act normal."

Flora shook her head. Yesterday, her mother was the one acting strange, and now she's telling Flora to act normal. Waiting for Verkin, Flora let Toros, Dickran and Nubar pass. Nubar slipped and fell on one knee. "Are you all right?" she asked and helped him to his feet.

"I'm fine." Nubar caught his breath. "Shouldn't you be taking care of your orphans?" He gave Flora a weak but loving smile. He trudged on, never complaining.

Flora admired his fortitude but realized how weak he had become. She grasped Verkin's hand and glanced over her shoulder at the young ones. Still in pairs, the orphans stayed close behind.

* * *

Carrying two sacks filled with food, Hagop warily watched soldiers busy with their preparations. No one paid any attention to him. He rushed across the street and merged into the column of exiles. Worried about his wife, he walked faster and hoped Arpi was still all right in her mind. Her strange behavior had occurred once before, years ago. He remembered she had returned to her rational self after eating an orange. Hmmm. The Turkish lady had given him an orange, yesterday, and he instinctively gave it to Arpi. Maybe he shouldn't give up on God yet. Then he saw the cluster of small children. Flora and Verkin were leading the ragged group.

Hagop gave Flora one of the sacks. "It's bulgur pilaf. Wait till the rest break." He walked ahead and took Arpi's hand.

"Thank God you're back," Arpi said. "I don't know what we would have done if you hadn't...."

"I know." Hagop put his arm around his wife's shoulder. "But I had to go. I think... God was with me."

CHAPTER TWENTY-ONE

A TASTE OF THE SYRIAN DESERT

Two hours later the terrain changed. All Flora could see was sand, miles of sand, her first taste of the Syrian Desert with its desolate face. No trees or shrubs. Only a narrow macadamized road for horses and carriages. The sun blazed. Her frayed shoes couldn't protect her feet against the burning sand.

A carriage passed by. The faces of the travelers on their way to Aleppo reflected disbelief as they watched the wretched column stretch into the horizon. Another carriage, rickety and slow moving, creaked along the broken tar road. Filtering down through the line of exiles, Flora heard voices call out the respectful salutation, *Catholicos*. She turned to see women making the sign of the cross as the dilapidated carriage passed by. Inside the shaking carriage was a tired old man with a white beard. He held a gold cross and blessed those he passed. It was The Catholigos Khabayan, Supreme Head of the Armenian Church of Cilicia. The muscles of his face twitched. When he saw the pitiful looking orphans, the Catholigos opened the door and motioned to the little ones. Six of them ran to him as he extended his hand to help them inside.

Out of the corner of her eye Flora saw Alai on his horse galloping toward the high priest. Four of the children ran back to the column, but two were already inside the carriage.

"No you don't!" Alai yelled and came to a halting stop in front of the Catholigos. He snapped his whip. "Get out," he screamed at the two children. The youngsters flew out of the carriage and rushed back to the column.

Alai glared at the Armenian holy man. "Go away, you *son of a bitch*. You're the head of these traitors!"

Flora thought the Catholigos might faint. Dazed, his face carried the signs of turmoil and agony as he closed the door. The carriage pulled away and faded into the dust. The Armenian Catholigos was powerless and couldn't help his people. Heads of religions in Turkey had for centuries carried the same prestige as ambassadors from great nations. They wielded great influence. *Not so for Armenians any longer*, Flora thought. *The Turks have severed us at our roots—our religion, our churches, our priests.* She glanced at her orphans and realized that *Armenia, too, was becoming an orphan.*

Warily, she turned to look for Alai. He was gone.

* * *

The sun was directly overhead. Time to rest. Flora watched as people slumped onto the hot, soft sand, like an endless line of falling dominos. She herded her little band of orphans close together. Some whimpered. Three of them held their bare feet and cried. They hadn't said anything about the heat till now. Flora tore the bottom of her skirt and wrapped their burned feet. They all needed water. How long could her father's water last? She puckered her cheeks remembering the wonderful sweet water in Hadjin that flowed with abundance. Her mouth was parched. She set the sack of pilaf on the sand beside her as she sat down. Her sister lay next to her. Verkin was exhausted.

"I'll take the pilaf," Hagop said. "We'll eat it tonight. He handed Flora small pieces of bread he had torn. "Give one to each of the children." He stared at Verkin. "Is she all right?"

"Let her sleep," Flora said. "I'll give them the bread." She hesitated. "What about water? We're all thirsty."

"I have to ration it."

As she handed each child a piece of bread, Flora watched as her father let a small amount of water slip into each of the children's mouths. When they reached the last child she said, "I feel like we're giving them communion." She wanted to laugh. "Maybe the bread will turn into fish."

"Don't joke about that."

Surprised and confused by her father's reaction, Flora watched as he picked up the sack of pilaf and walk over to her mother. He held the water bag up to Arpi's mouth and Flora, wanting her share, rushed to her father's side. As the water trickled from the leather bag into her mouth, Flora savored every drop. When her father pulled the bag away, she wondered when they would find water. A pang of fear shot through her. *What if there is no water in the desert?*

* * *

Hours later, when the convoy stopped to camp for the evening, Hagop gave Flora the sack containing the pilaf. "Ration it."

"How?"

"If each child takes only a handful, the bigger ones will get more for their bigger bodies. We adults will wait."

"I hope there's enough to go around," Flora said opening the sack.

"Me, too," Hagop responded.

Flora turned to see the children waiting patiently. "Line up with your partner," she said.

Scurrying, the children rushed and stood in front of her. No one pushed or tried to get ahead.

"Take only what one hand will hold...and no more." Flora held the bag open and watched each child take the meager ration. She felt it remarkable none of them grabbed, knowing every one of them wanted to eat and eat until their stomachs were full. Miss Webb would have been proud of them. They were so good. She handed the remaining pilaf to her father. He divided the precious food, Dickran and Avedis getting their share first.

Flora licked every morsel of grain off her dirty fingers, recalling how she used to help her mother thresh wheat in her yard at home and shoo away the crows who'd swoop down trying to steal the fresh grain. She remembered the wonderful Sunday dinners after church and yearned for those happy days to return.

The sun, golden-red and huge, dipped and spread pink rays across the yellow sand. Flora gazed across the vast plain, watching the silhouette of a camel caravan passing in the distance. Sensing a unique quiet, she understood why saints choose to spend time in the barren desert. Its beauty moved her. She wanted to understand its secrets. Why was it so barren? Was it undergoing a spiritual transformation where it had to be immaculately clean before it could or would let anything grow? She watched the sun disappear behind a mound of sand and in that instant felt an overwhelming love flood over her. It was as if a mellow light of joy surrounded her. Never before had she felt anything so wonderful. She looked up into the heavens. *Is this a sign from God,* she wondered. *Is He trying to tell me He is real?* Engulfed with joyous love she reached for her Bible, wanting to read scripture. This mighty love had something to do with the orphans, but she wasn't quite sure what. She just knew she had a strong connection to these young souls. Maybe it had something to do with her own fear of becoming an orphan. Searching her mind for a passage that would relate to the children, she opened the Holy Book. It opened to Luke, in the middle of chapter six.

Huddled together, the haggard children sat quietly, watching her. She walked toward them, and they smiled. Leading them in the Lord's Prayer, she asked God to shower blessings upon all the Hadjin missionaries, especially Miss Webb. Then she read from the scriptures, pouring her own love into the words. Surprised how the children comprehended the part about the hungry being filled, Flora felt her own heart swelling with happiness.

Later, as the night grew cold, Flora couldn't sleep. She gazed into the dark sky, the stars shimmering and twinkling as if they were saying "Hello, little Flora. She couldn't fathom the immensity of it all. *What purpose could she possibly have in this huge universe? Something with the orphans?*

As night gave way to the light of dawn, Flora shivered and snuggled closer to her sister. Still feeling yesterday's bubble of love surrounding her, she smiled and looked toward the orphans. Some were beginning to stir. One by one they sat up as the sun displayed its golden rays. She stood up and rubbed her arms.

The children walked toward her saying, "Morning Flora," or "Flora," or just "Morning." She put her arm around each as they approached, knowing the powerful gift of love she mysteriously received was to be shared with these little ones. Her eyes fell on three-year-old Vartan. He was so frail. But so were all the others. She felt responsible for their safety. Why? She didn't really know, but it had something to do with yesterday's spiritual experience.

Masses of sleeping bodies stirred. People sat pressed together trying to keep warm. At midday the heat from the sun would be relentless, and they would wish for the coolness of the desert morning. It was 6 a.m. An hour later the convict-gendarmes and the two soldiers appeared. They stood in the middle of the road and waited. The Hadjin exiles began to line up.

Flora picked up Vartan and carried him the entire day, some of his lice finding their way into her hair. But she thought only of what she perceived as her sign from God. The joyous love surrounding her was not like the love she felt from her father, mother or Miss Webb. It was a thousand times stronger. She'd never forget it, nor would she ever tell anyone about it. It affected her too deeply. The energizing joy had carried her through the hardships of the last two days—her hunger and thirst, the intense heat and the incredibly cold nights—she seemed to be beyond it. She couldn't explain it.

CHAPTER TWENTY-TWO

KATMA

When the convoy reached Katma, a village on the outskirts of Aleppo, Flora flinched when she saw the field behind the Katma railroad station. An ocean of humans, as far as she could see, had camped near the station. Wilted from the sun's penetrating hot rays, thousands lay everywhere. No trees and no shade. Here and there a few bed sheets, carpets, and clothes were propped up to keep away the sun's burning rays. Flora's heart sank as she followed her father into the camp. A peculiar musty odor worried her. Languid people with congested eyes and rashes were everywhere. "Father?"

"I think it's typhus," Hagop said.

Just then Nubar collapsed.

"We'll go no farther," Hagop said as he tried to make his friend comfortable.

"It would be easier for me to die here," Nubar said, closing his eyes and falling into a heavy sleep.

Toros helped his father make a lean-to with a camel skin to protect Nubar from the sun. Flora covered Nubar with a blanket. She didn't want him to die. He was more than her father's business partner and friend. He was like an uncle. She said a silent prayer for him and then organized the orphans as best she could. She worried for them, too. Typhus meant death. Everyone feared it. Now it was among them.

She sat with the children and watched another convoy leave the camp. That confused her. It was late afternoon. Meanwhile, other gendarmes walked along the perimeter guarding the Armenian exiles. *Why bother? Where could we go? Who would dare give us asylum or shelter?*

Anyone caught helping an Armenian would be deported—or worse.

* * *

Alai, Haidar, and the four convict-gendarmes watched their convoy enter the crowded camp as another group filed out. A carriage pulled up and stopped beside Alai. Inside was a Turkish officer, sickly looking and pale, a skeleton that glanced out the window at the multitudes of Armenians. "Who are those people in that field?"

"Armenians," Alai said.

"Armenians! Are there still Armenians living in this part of our fatherland?"

Alai smiled. "For the moment." He paused, looked at the four convict-gendarmes and turned to the Turkish officer. "Sir, are you on your way to Aleppo?

"Yes. I'm on leave-of-absence from Van." He couldn't keep his eyes off the field choked with listless bodies. "I didn't see a single living Armenian in any of the towns I passed through. Why have they left these serpents alive? They should be exterminated! The traitors!"

Alai dismounted, held the reins and walked closer to the Turkish officer. "Sir, these poor gendarmes have felt humiliated walking alongside the traitors to our fatherland. Will you allow these good, tired Turks to travel to Aleppo with you? We are to report to General Jemal Pasha at the Baron Hotel."

"Jemal! Of course they can ride with me." He scanned the six Turks. "You all need to clean up before you see the General!"

"Thank you, Captain," Alai said. He saluted, then turned to the four convicts and pointed to the carriage.

They hesitated.

Alai put his hand on his rifle, and the convicts rushed into the carriage.

Remounting his horse, Alai followed the carriage as it pulled away toward Aleppo.

"Now we'll know exactly where they are," Haidar said. "Once they report to the general we'll be safe."

"You bet," Alai responded. "I don't intend to die so they can disappear into the city and live an easy life." He rubbed his neck, remembering the hanging threat.

CHAPTER TWENTY-THREE

A HORRENDOUS DECISION

Near the gate of the Katma camp was a man dressed in an Arabic galabiya and headdress. Flora watched the man as his wily hands moved in rhythm with his fast moving mouth. Acting as if he were important, he showed papers to the gate guard. The man, about her father's age, strode into the camp, his eyes searching. Then he shouted in Turkish, "Protestants! Who's a Protestant? I have come to take you away." His voice sang, as if he were selling lemonade.

Hesitating, Flora wanted to run to him, tell him she had twenty Protestant orphans, but who was he? Could she trust him? What if he wanted children to sell? His face had Armenian features, a big nose and bushy eyebrow, and she overheard him whisper in Armenian to a woman, "Aren't you Protestant?"

Flora cautiously approached him. "*Baron*, Mister, why are you looking for Protestants?

"There is a new directive for Protestants, but I can't find anyone who'll say they are." He raised his arms in disbelief.

"I have twenty from the Hadjin orphanage."

"Take me to them."

Flora brought the man to her father.

"Hovaness Juskalian," the man said introducing himself to Hagop.

"You're not Arab?" Hagop asked.

"No, but I've lived among Arabs all my life. I'm helping Reverend Eskijian, the Protestant minister in Aleppo." He adjusted his headdress and said. "My Arabic attire makes my work for him easier."

"Why are you looking for Protestants?" Flora asked, looking up at the six-foot man. "Is it true they are no longer exiled?"

"Supposedly so, young lady." Hovaness brushed his hand over Flora's head. "But it's dangerous for any Armenian to return to Turkey." He turned to Hagop. "We are telling them to go on to

Damascus. Everyone else is being sent to the desert at Der-el-Zor... that's the worst place to go."

"The Allies? Are they winning in the Dardanelles?" Hagop asked and shifted nervously. "Their victory will save us."

"The Turks are putting up a strong defense."

"Oh God, No!"

"It doesn't look like the Allies will make it to Constantinople."

"That's terrible news for us," Hagop said. "What hope do we have now?"

Hovaness took a deep breath. "The longer the war lasts, the worse it is for us Armenians. The Reverend is afraid Armenia is doomed to extinction." He gazed at the twenty ragged orphans. "He says our only hope for Armenia is to save the young ones... like these little ones."

"You'll take all twenty?" Hagop asked.

"The Reverend will be overwhelmed, but, yes, I'll take them all." He pointed to a wagon parked by the road. "There's room for maybe ten or twelve in the wagon. The older ones will walk."

"I'd like to say a prayer with them," Flora said. Bible in hand she walked to the children and prayed with them, asking God to look after them, to give blessings to the Hadjin missionaries and to Baron Hovaness, who, by the Grace of God, was going to take them to safety.

"Bye, Flora, bye." They waved as they followed Mr. Hovaness. Little, frail Vartan ran to Flora and hugged her leg with all his might. Flora lifted him, kissed his cheek, and set him down.

"I want to stay with you, Flora. I love you," Vartan said, brushing the tears from his eyes.

"No, Vartan. You must go with the others. I know it's God's wish for you." Flora patted his little bottom. "Now go!" Vartan hesitated. "Go!" Vartan hugged her leg again, and Flora watched him run after the others. The bubble of love that had surrounded her for three days burst, like a light going out. "I've done my job," she said to herself and wondered what would have happened to them if she and her father hadn't intervened.

* * *

Late the next afternoon Alai and Haidar, in clean uniforms with rifles strapped to their backs, sat on fresh horses waiting at the camp's entrance. Two new soldiers accompanied them, and they appeared to have more authority than the convict-gendarmes. Then came the dreaded words, "All from Hadjin, come!"

Hagop considered not responding but knew the consequences would be disastrous. He sensed a new pattern in moving the convoys and wanted to laugh at what he assumed was a Turkish consideration for the exhausted deportees. Now the deportees would be allowed to rest during the heat of the day and start their forced march just before sundown.

He bent to pick up a camel skin and heard a faint voice in his head. He thought the words said, "The girls are in danger." It sounded like his mother's voice. He shook his head thinking it had to be his imagination, but then again maybe not. From the time he could remember his mother had unusual ways, and she could be trying to warn him. He glared at the two vile soldiers. Yes, he thought, *they are to be feared* and the fear surged through his spine and into the back of his skull. His body trembled. He needed moral support from Nubar, but realized his good friend needed his help. "Will you be able to walk?" he asked Nubar.

Nubar stood and steadied himself. He had slept for almost two full days. "I'll be all right." His voice was weak.

Hagop put Nubar's arm around his shoulder, held his waist, and helped him merge into the growing column of Hadjin exiles.

Toros approached his father. "Let me help."

"No. Stay with Mother. Verkin, you carry Avedis." Dickran had already grasped Flora's hand. They left the camp and soon thereafter nothing was ahead but soft sand. The heat of the day had passed, but it was still warm.

Leaning against Hagop, Nubar said, "You and I both know the Turks will eventually kill us, but the girls' fates...." He stumbled. "If Verkin and Flora escape the lusting of these degenerate soldiers, they'll either be sold to the white slave market or to a Turk for his harem." Nubar tried to take a deep breath, his voice barely audible.

"Why not leave them in Aleppo? It could be their only chance to survive."

Hagop didn't answer. Feeling Nubar slip, he gripped his friend's waist more tightly. His eyes fell on his two daughters. Verkin's beautiful blue eyes were now dull. Flora, his wonderful Flora, who was so caring toward the orphans, who was so full of life, what will happen to her? Could he leave them? Who'd watch over them? Arpi would be devastated. So would he. Not knowing if his daughters would survive was excruciating. *But that voice.* Was it a warning from his dead mother?

He wrestled with the heavy thoughts in his mind. Finally, he made a decision.

***

The Hadjin convoy reached the outskirts of Aleppo, a modern, bustling Arab city with 130,000 inhabitants. Built in the middle of the desert, it was a popular caravan route to Afghanistan and India. Minarets stretched high above roofs of sprawling buildings and homes. Golden ribbons of light from the setting sun fell on the ancient fortress standing on top of the only hill in the city. Men dressed in *galabias* and the traditional Arab headdress rushed through the streets. Most stopped to look as the convoy neared. It was unusual for a convoy on its way to Del-el-Zor to be so close to the city.

Hagop noticed the compassionate eyes of the Arab men watching the wretched group trudging along. Should he act now? He hesitated. What if he failed? Noticing a shoemaker closing his shop, Hagop reacted and charged ahead. The man looked Armenian. "My two girls," he said in Armenian, "please, save them from the Turks."

The man jumped, startled.

His eyes pleading, Hagop gestured toward the convoy and to Flora and Verkin.

The man glanced at the two ragged girls and studied a tearful Hagop. "I'll take them to Reverend Eskijian."

"The Protestant minister?"

"Yes."

"Thank you," Hagop said choking. "God bless you." He rushed back to his girls. "That man will take both of you to the Protestant minister. If and when the Turks release us, we'll know where to find you."

Verkin froze.

Flora burst into tears. "I don't want to leave you."

"I know what's best." Hagop took their hands and said, "Quickly!"

Watching Hagop rush away with the girls, Nubar mustered up his strength and stumbled in the opposite direction. He shrieked, "I can't go on anymore! I can't walk anymore!"

Alai pulled the reins of his horse and turned around. He rode toward Nubar and slowly circled him.

Nubar shook his fist. "Are you going to kill me?"

Alai played with his whip as he continued to circle Nubar. "If you can't go on, you can expect a taste of this!" He snapped the whip in the air. His birthmark deepened red.

Nubar covered his head with his skinny arms and dropped to his knees.

Crack! Crack!

Nubar fell flat. Blood spewed from his back.

"Get up!"

Nubar couldn't move.

Alai dismounted. "Get up!" he said, and then lashed the whip on Nubar's back over and over and over.

At that moment Hagop handed his daughters to the Armenian man, who snatched their hands and ran away.

His feet wide apart, a breathless Alai raised his whip high in the air. "Any more can't go on?"

Petrified women and children rushed on, pushing their exhausted bodies.

Alai remounted his horse and rode back to the head of the convoy, a smile spreading across his face.

Hagop ran to Nubar. Bending down he whispered, "Thank you, old friend. You have given my girls a chance."

He tried to lift Nubar out of the pool of blood. "Try to stand." Hagop was covered with blood.

"No. Leave me. I want death to take me today." He coughed. "I wish I understood why the Turks have done this awful thing." Those were the last words he spoke. He gasped and closed his eyes.

Hagop tried to control his tears but they flowed like a swift river. His eyes burned. He embraced Nubar, shook with intense anger and sobbed. "I wish I understood, too." He had lost both his daughters and his best friend in a matter of minutes.

He kissed his friend on the forehead and stood, his knees weak. He walked with a sluggish gait to his wife and put his blood soaked arm around her. "I didn't have a choice."

"I know," Arpi said, stunned. "My girls, my girls." She wept hopelessly.

"God forgive me." Hagop picked up Avedis. His son was trembling.

Dickran reached for his mother's hand. His other hand grasped Toros' leg.

They did not look back.

TWENTY FOUR

TRAUMATIZED

The shoemaker ducked into an alley. Dropping the girls' hands, he said, "My wife and I will be deported if a gendarme catches me." His breath was noisy. "Wait here." Rushing to the end of the alley, he spotted two Arab men walking together in the residential area. An old woman wearing the traditional black *chador* sat in a chair crocheting. She picked up her yarn and hobbled up the stairs into her home. Otherwise, the street was clear. "Stay behind me," he said and charged ahead.

Hurrying to keep up, Flora clutched her Bible as tears streamed down her face. Verkin was also crying.

The man turned down two more streets, rushed through another alley and into a narrow lane. Hastily scanning the area, he ran to a house, opened the door, waited for the girls, and pulled them inside.

"Haig, why are you so late?" a voice called. "Supper is cold." A woman walked into the living room, stopped, and the smile on her face vanished as she eyed the two ragged girls. "Who are they?"

Haig did not answer.

She addressed Verkin. "From one of the convoys?"

"Yes." Verkin's voice cracked. "From Hadjin."

The woman scowled. "Haig!"

"The *Badveli*, (Reverend), said we should help," Haig said, stretching his arms toward the picture of Christ that hung on the wall.

"Come into the kitchen." The woman stormed out of the room.

Turning toward the girls, Haig made an attempt to smile. "Everything will be all right." He walked away as if he didn't want to face his wife. His feet barely touched the floor.

Whispering sounds filtered from the kitchen.

Exhausted, both Flora and Verkin glanced at the chairs and the cushioned bench along one of the walls in the living room. Neither made an effort to sit.

"They can't stay!" the woman shouted.

"Shhh."

The voices reverted to soft murmurs.

Five minutes later, Haig returned and slumped into one of the chairs. "Forgive my wife. You must know how dangerous it is to help." He pointed to the bench and said, "Sit down. You must be tired."

"We're too dirty," Flora said.

"Yes," he nodded and rose from his comfortable chair. "My wife wouldn't like it. Come. Come and wash."

Entering the kitchen, both girls' eyes widened. The sight and smell of the stew on the table overwhelmed them. Flora noticed chucks of meat in the bowls. Were they pieces of lamb? Her mouth was parched, but she felt saliva forming. Not able to remember the last time she had eaten even a morsel of meat, she wanted to devour all of it immediately, but Haig's wife pointed to a basin filled with water.

She and Verkin hurried to the counter and washed.

"Please, sit," Haig's wife said, her voice now calm.

Hands and faces clean, Flora and Verkin rushed to the table, sat, crossed themselves, and in between quick breaths scoffed down the hot meal.

"Thank you, Mrs...." Flora said and stopped.

"Balian, Ani Balian."

"Thank you, Mrs. Balian."

"Yes," Verkin said. "We haven't eaten for days."

"Nor has the rest of our family," Flora said as tears flowed down her cheeks.

"Poor child." Mr. Balian shifted nervously and as he left the room he said, "Ani, I'll heat water for their bath."

Mrs. Balian placed her hands on the girls' shoulders. "We'll have clothes for you in the morning, too." She patted Flora's back. "Tomorrow my husband will take you to the *Badveli*. He'll find good homes for both of you."

Flora managed a grateful smile, but felt anxious. This was her first night away from her family and the protection of her father.

"One bath is ready," Haig called out.

* * *

Clean, warm and comfortable the girls lay together on a folding mattress in the front room. Stomachs full, they closed their eyes but neither could sleep. Flora snuggled up to Verkin and kissed her. She had a gnawing fear she'd never see the rest of her family again.

"Go to sleep," Verkin said and brushed her hand over Flora's damp eyes.

Flora nodded, but her mind was racing. Where were her parents? Never had she been out of their sight, except for that time in Constantinople, but then Miss Webb was like another mother. She hated not being with her parents. But she knew it was dangerous for her or her sister to be within Alai's grasp. Unsteady and unsafe, Flora felt as if she were adrift in the middle of an ocean and thought that orphans always felt that way. She wondered about Vartan, Mary, and the others, and the love she felt when she was near them. And where were Ana and Sona? She thought about her talented friends who'd no longer have the opportunity to create wonderful music, and knew they were in the clutches of the pock-faced man and were being forced in harlotry.

Listening to her sister's rhythmic breathing, Flora snuggled closer, needing to feel Verkin's body against hers. She wondered about Nubar. Was he all right? She shivered and forced herself not to burst into a sob. Finally her mind drifted into dark and unsettled oblivion.

* * *

The next morning at dawn Flora opened her eyes to see Mrs. Balian standing by her and Verkin. She held two black dresses similar to Moslem *chadors* in her hands. Mrs. Balian dropped the plain black dresses and a *charshaf* on each girl. "Today, you'll dress as Moslems."

Walking toward the kitchen, she said, "Breakfast will be ready soon."

Flora fingered the dress resting on her belly. "Well," she said as she threw the dress on top of her sister, "It's not a fashionable Paris design."

Verkin chuckled, sat up and compared the dresses. "They look exactly the same to me. Which one do you want?"

"The shorter one, dummy!" Flora reached to take the dress and instead lunged for her sister. She hugged Verkin so hard, she thought what little flesh she had left on her bones would melt. "I'm so scared," she sobbed.

They stayed locked together for a full minute, Flora trembling the whole time.

"We've got each other," Verkin said and lifted Flora's head. She gently caressed her sister's eyes.

Flora pressed her lips together.

"Girls," Mrs. Balian called. "Milk is hot."

"We'll be right there," Verkin said and whispered, "Will you be all right?" and when Flora nodded, Verkin said, "Hurry."

They scrambled, folding the blanket and mattress. They threw on their non-Parisian fashions, tied the *charshafs* around their heads and went into the kitchen.

Already sitting at the table was Mr. Balian. He smiled. "You look like two wonderful young Moslem girls. The Reverend will be happy you're converting!"

Mrs. Balian chuckled and put four bowls of hot oats on the table, then, said a blessing.

Gratefully, Flora ate her share, licked her lips, and remembered how she wouldn't touch oatmeal when there was plenty to eat back home, when the thought of not having an abundance of food every day had never before entered her young mind.

"Girls," Mr. Balian said, "Reverend Eskijian's church is a long walk from here. If a gendarme or a soldier stops me for my papers, you must keep going. Don't worry. They don't bother Moslem women." He stood. "For God's sake, whatever you do, don't speak Armenian to anyone until you are in the Reverend's compound!"

Picking up her Bible, Flora said, "I speak Turkish."

"That's better than Armenian, but most Arabs don't speak Turkish. The sooner you learn Arabic, the safer you'll be." Haig stood. "Time to go." He walked into the living room, and the girls followed.

Haig opened the door. "Bye, Ani."

Ani rushed into the room. She brushed her hand along her husband's cheek. "Be careful, Haig."

"Of course."

"Thank you, Mrs. Balian," Flora and Verkin said in unison.

"The *Badveli* will find good homes for you."

"We must go," Haig said. "Girls, don't forget what I told you. Stay a good distance behind me. If I'm stopped, keep walking and turn down the first alley you see. I'll find you." He rubbed his damp forehead and rushed off.

Ani held back the girls until her husband was half way up the street. "Go now." She gently pushed the girls out the door and closed it.

Hearing the click locking the door, Flora felt as if she had been abandoned, not knowing where to go or how to get there. Her hands clammy, she grasped Verkin's hand, but kept her eyes fixed on Mr. Balian.

He turned down a street and disappeared.

The two girls hurried, turned down the next street, and immediately froze. Three Turkish soldiers on horses rode toward them.

Haig had stopped, his back turned to the soldiers. He pulled a cigarette from the package in his pocket, lit it and covered half his face with his cupped hands.

Flora wrapped the outside of her skirt around her Bible. What would the soldiers think if they saw a Moslem carrying a Christian Bible? Increasing her pace, she pulled Verkin and kept her eyes focused on the ground.

They passed Haig as he threw the lighted match to the ground.

"Stay calm," Haig whispered and casually blew out the cigarette smoke.

The girls slowed down.

A soldier rode toward Haig and stopped. "Do you speak Turkish?"

Haig shook his head. "*Effendi*, no."

"Baron Hotel? Where?" the soldier asked.

Haig took another drag from his cigarette, pointed straight ahead, and watched the soldiers ride away. He hurried and turned into the first alley.

The girls stood, waiting, fear in their eyes.

"They're gone," he said.

Too scared to respond, Flora nodded.

"Follow me." Haig zigzagged through streets and alleys in the residential area. A well-dressed European passed by in an open carriage. Two men wearing loose fitting *galabias*, their donkeys laden with goods to sell at Aleppo's covered bazaar walked in the middle of the treeless street. Only a few trees loomed here and there to provide shade or greenery in the sand colored desert city.

Haig rushed down two more streets and stopped in front of a large compound. He opened a gate and motioned for the girls to follow. He disappeared inside.

The girls ran through the open gate and slammed it shut. Flora's heart sank. The ground was covered with people, some still sleeping. Was this just another refugee camp? She quickly scanned the courtyard. Secured by a high fence, three sides of the squared area were occupied by a church, a house, and a building. Was the building an orphanage? Her Hadjin orphans. Were they here?

Already on the porch, Haig knocked at the front door of the house. The girls raced up the stairs and stood beside him.

A man with brown hair, kind brown eyes and a bushy mustache opened the door. He was in his mid-thirties and looked tired.

"Reverend, I have two girls from the Hadjin convoy."

"Come in, Haig." He smiled at the two girls in Moslem attire. "You, too," he said and closed the door behind them.

Standing in the hallway, Flora noticed the fine furniture in the living room. The shiny, grand piano reminded her of Sona.

"Please, sit down." The Reverend pointed toward two elegant French style chairs.

The girls responded to his kind gesture, entered the room, sat and waited.

"We'll be back shortly," the Reverend said as he and Haig left the girls.

Sitting beside the piano, Flora wanted to touch it. How happy Sona would have been to sit at this fine piano and play one of her Beethoven sonatas. Flora felt sad. She knew her talented friend would never again sit in front of a piano.

Haig and the pastor returned within minutes. "The Reverend says you can spend the night here. Sometimes young Armenian girls can be placed with families looking for domestic help."

Flora didn't know how to react. She knew she should be grateful for escaping from the convoy, but she didn't want to be a servant. Being a servant was the lowliest job anyone could have in Hadjin.

"I should be able to find you a home by tomorrow," the Reverend said.

"I'd offer mine, but my wife becomes a nervous wreck whenever a Turkish soldier or gendarme enters our street," Haig said.

"We understand," Verkin said.

"Thank you, Mr. Balian," Flora said.

"Goodbye and good luck." Haig opened the front door and immediately slammed it shut. "Gendarmes!"

"Quickly!" The Reverend grabbed the girls' hands and ran to the kitchen. He pushed aside the table, pulled the carpet and lifted a door cut into the floor. "Hide down there!"

Flora and Verkin scrambled down the small ladder. The door slammed shut. Table legs screeched. Flora held her breath. When her eyes adjusted, she was on top of a bed of charcoal. She reached for Verkin. Her sister's hand was clammy.

Dust floated into her nostrils. She felt a sneeze, squeezed her nostrils hard and sat frozen still.

Overhead footsteps rushed through the kitchen, a door opened, and sounds of heavy feet climbed stairs.

Flora took a breath through her mouth. Her eyes closed tight, she rubbed and rubbed her nostrils. The sneeze dissipated.

Neither girl dared move. Time dragged. More than an hour passed when finally a crack of light filtered through the overhead door as it squeaked open.

A woman peered through the hole.

"It's safe." She extended her arm. "Come."

Flora reached for her hand and climbed up. Relieved to be out of the dark hole, she watched as the woman helped her sister. Verkin was covered with coal dust.

"I'm the Reverend's wife," the woman said.

The girls merely nodded. They had not yet recovered from the dread of the last hour. Flora removed her charshaf and scanned the cozy kitchen.

Two young boys in sleeping shirts stood quietly in the doorway. They were about the same ages as Avedis and Dickran.

"My sons," the Reverend's wife said and motioned for the boys to come closer.

The Reverend entered the kitchen and brushed his hands through their hair. "Get dressed."

The two boys scooted out of the room.

"I didn't know about this raid," the Reverend said and handed each girl a cloth wet with warm water. "Otherwise we would have had the refugees scatter to hide elsewhere. My contacts usually inform me when the gendarmes are coming to look for escaped Armenians."

"Like us?" Flora asked as she wiped the dust off her face and hands.

The Reverend nodded.

"What happens when the gendarmes find them… or us?" Verkin asked holding her breath.

The Reverend lowered his eyes. "The gendarmes escort them to a convoy headed to the desert at Der-el-Zor."

Der-el-Zor. Flora knew what that meant. It was a death warrant.

Mrs. Eskijian set a glass of warm milk on the table. "Sit down, please."

Flora placed her hands around the warm glass. She took two sips, savoring the taste and turned to the Reverend. "Mr. Balian, is he safe?"

"Yes," he said, a half smile forming. "He always carries papers that says he's a resident of Aleppo."

The girls gulped their milk.

"Now, tell me your names."

Verkin took off her charshaf. "Verkin Munushian."

"And I'm Flora Munushian."

"Your ages?"

"I'm sixteen," Verkin said.

"And I'm fourteen."

"Hmmm. You look younger, but I should be able to find domestic work for you both.

Flora blinked, hating the thought of becoming a servant. She had had such great dreams for herself. Thinking about her orphans, she wondered if they, too, would become servants. She turned to the minister. "Do you know a Mr. Hovaness?"

"Yes. How do you know him?"

"He came to the camp at Katma and took twenty of our Hadjin orphans."

Reverend Eskijian's eyes lit up. "You're that Flora!"

Both Verkin and Flora smiled.

"Yes, she is," Verkin said.

"I expected someone much older. They talk about you constantly."

"Then they're here?" Flora asked.

"Yes," but the older ones are being taken to the German orphanage this afternoon."

"The Germans?" Flora gasped.

"German missionaries are helping too," the Reverend said.

"Can I see them?"

The Reverend opened a door. "Follow me." He escorted the girls upstairs to the second floor, opened another door and walked into a room full of children.

A voice shrieked. "It's Flora!" The youngster ran to Flora and hugged her leg. It was Vartan. His head was shaved.

Flora picked him up, smelling kerosene on his head. "What happened to your hair?"

"Full of bugs."

More bald-looking children ran to her. "Flora, Flora," they cried and gathered around.

Setting Vartan down, Flora reached out to touch them and felt that familiar glowing love surround her again.

"Hello, Verkin." Mary, the eldest of the group, pulled at Verkin's skirt.

Verkin hugged her.

"Did you become Moslem?" Mary asked.

"No," Verkin laughed. "It's a long story."

The Reverend went to talk to the matron in charge. Returning, he said to the girls, "You can spend the night here. It'll be safe today. The gendarmes have already raided us." He gazed out the window into the empty courtyard.

"Thank you," Verkin said.

Flora echoed her sister's gratitude. Her arms stretched around two of the orphans, as she watched the Reverend walk down the stairs. Even his footsteps sounded tired. The man was exhausted, and his day was just beginning. Her heart went out to him.

He helped so many.

TWENTY-FIVE

A RELATION APPEARS

Tears streamed down Flora's face when she lay down to sleep that night. Questions plagued her mind. *What is to be our fate? Will we be separated?* She wanted desperately to stay with Verkin. *Will a good family take both of us? Where are my parents? And my brothers? Are they all right?* Finally, she could cry no more and her exhausted body fell into a deep slumber.

Still at the orphanage four days later and not wanting her orphans to see her pain, Flora managed to keep a smile on her face. She found it hard to say goodbye to the nine older ones who were being taken to the German orphanage today. There they'd have a chance to survive. Turkish gendarmes seldom patrolled the German orphanage.

There was so much pain everywhere. She knew she was not alone, but still it was hard for her to accept that her secure life was taken away. She noticed Baron Hovaness entering the compound. Still dressed in Arab attire and carrying bags of bread, he handed the small loaves to the ragged refugees who had found their way to the compound. There was not enough for everyone.

Pressing her nose against the window, she saw a familiar face. "Verkin, that can't be Siran! Is it?" Flora blurted out.

Verkin hurried to the window. "My God. It is!"

Their twenty-two-year-old cousin and her son stood out among the ragged refugees in the courtyard. They were clean.

Rushing down the stairs and out into the courtyard, Flora and Verkin yelled, "Siran!"

Stunned, Siran embraced both girls. Tears streamed down her face.

"How did you get here? Where's your mother and father? Do you know anything about my family?" Flora asked as she lifted and hugged young Krikor.

"Slow down, Flora," Siran responded.

"With the Arabs," Krikor said as Flora set him down. "They are with the Arabs."

"Arabs?" Verkin asked.

"Yes. Everything happened so fast," Siran said.

"You weren't in a convoy?"

"We were, but when we got to Katma, Father showed an Arab a fist full of money. The Arab came back that night with a wagon and took us to his village."

"Where are your mother and father now? And your other son?" Verkin asked.

"In the Arab's village. God, I hope they'll be all right." Siran wiped away the tear that rolled down her cheek.

"How did you get here. And why did you leave?" Flora asked.

"The chief of the village said I had to marry him!"

"My God," Verkin said. "Didn't he know you already had a husband and two children."

"He didn't care. We couldn't make him understand that my husband was in America waiting for me." Her eyes fell on her son.

"Now we'll never get there." Siran began to laugh, her laughter growing louder as her head started shaking.

Flora took hold of Siran and shook her. "Stop it!"

Siran burst into tears and collapsed on the dirt.

Krikor kneeled down and wiped the tears from his mother's cheeks. "I'll take care of you, Mother."

Flora helped Siran to her feet.

Siran quickly regained her composure. "Father bribed another Arab to secretly bring us to Aleppo. My mother said to leave my two-year old with them. Said he'd be safer there." Siran glanced through the compound. "Where is your family? Are they here?"

"On their way to Der-el-Zor," Verkin said. "Grandmother died in Memoreh."

Siran's eyes welled.

"And the Turks took Levon," Flora said. Staring at all the refugees in the compound, she added, "God knows how long the rest of us can survive."

"Flora! Verkin!" the Reverend called out from the porch.

"I'll mention you to the Reverend," Flora said. "Maybe he can find you a job." She and Verkin dashed away and ran up the stairs onto the porch.

"Come inside," the Reverend said. The girls followed him into the living room where two men and a woman sat, waiting.

The woman stood, as did the man sitting next to her. An older couple, their fine attire spoke of economic means.

"Verkin, this is Mrs. Shar and her husband, Michel. They'll take you to their home."

A huge smile crossed Mrs. Shar's pleasant face. The woman reached to take Verkin's hands.

Verkin hesitated.

The Reverend placed his hand on Verkin's back and gently pushed until she was within reach. "The Shars are anxious to have you live with them. They don't have children."

Verkin touched Mrs. Shar's hands, but quickly let go.

Turning to Flora, the Reverend said, "Mr. Andonian will take you home."

Mr. Andonian stood.

Flora was surprised he was so short. He looked much taller sitting in the chair and his wrinkled trousers told her he was not from high culture.

A grin spread across Mr. Andonian's face. He looked amused.

Flora felt her blood run cold. She didn't want to go with him. But, why? It wasn't the man's looks. His olive face and big nose was typically Armenian, but that grin and something about his manner bothered her. Did she dare tell the Reverend, who was so good and overworked and lived an exemplary Christian life? He helped every refugee who came to his door. How could she complain? Anyway, the Pastor wouldn't send her into a dangerous situation, but Mr. Andonian repulsed her, and the man hadn't said a word.

Flora took a deep breath. "I'd like to say good-bye to the Hadjin orphans."

"Me, too," Verkin added.

"Of course. They'll be sad to see you go," the Reverend said.

"Please excuse us," Flora said and took her sister's hand. The two girls walked into the kitchen. Flora opened the orphanage door, slammed it shut behind her and fell back against it. Trembling, she said, "I don't want to leave you. I don't want to live with Mr. Andonian."

"We don't have a choice," Verkin said.

Der-el-Zor loomed in Flora's mind. *If I don't go with Mr. Andonian, how long can I evade the gendarmes?* She could hear her heart pounding as she followed her sister up the stairs.

Children sat in small groups making rugs, spinning wool or learning Armenian and Arabic scripts. Her orphans, all of them bald, sat around a teacher reading them a story.

Flora and Verkin stood and waited. Vartan's face lit into a bright smile, and he pushed himself up and ran to Flora.

"Fuzz. Your hair is growing back," Flora said and brushed her hand over his head. "We came to say good-bye. The Reverend found us a home."

The children sat silent. "We'll miss you," one of them said.

"Yes, yes, yes," several repeated.

Tears welled in Vartan's eyes.

Flora picked up the three-year-old. "We'll come to church on Sundays. We'll see each other."

Vartan put his arms around Flora's neck and hugged her.

Flora set him down, giving him a long, loving look. "Bye."

"Till Sunday," Verkin said to the children.

Flora took a last look at the little faces who sat like small birds not wanting their mother to leave their nest and wondered what was her mystical connection with them. Turning away, she and her sister picked up the two black chadors. Flora cradled her Bible against her chest.

The matron approached holding two woolen shawls. "These will keep you warm."

"Thank you," Verkin said, taking the white one.

The matron handed Flora the brown one.

"Go with God," she said.

Unable to smile Flora followed Verkin through the open door and down the stairs. Entering the living room, Flora made a beeline for the Pastor. "We'll be able to attend church on Sundays, won't we?" She immediately turned to face Mr. Andonian, as if on a dare, and heard the reverend's warm words.

"Of course."

Mr. Andonian's nod was tentative. He looked uneasy.

Flora fastened her defiant eyes on the man who was to take her away today. She wanted to express her fears to the reverend, but didn't have the heart to upset him. Instead, she thanked him for helping her, her sister, and all the refugees. She wanted to hug the kind reverend, but felt it improper. After all, he was a man of God.

When the small group gathered on the porch, Flora noticed her cousin rushing toward them.

"I almost forgot," Flora exclaimed. "My cousin, Siran, escaped from an Arab chief who wanted to marry her."

"You must be Reverend Eskijian," Siran said as she hurried up the three stairs and introduced herself and her son, Krikor, who held onto his mother's hand as if he'd never let go. Siran swung Krikor in front and grasped him with both arms. "I must take care of my son. Do you have a job for me?"

"She has a good education," Flora said. Could she be a teacher in the orphanage?"

The Reverend sighed. "There are so many who need work. I'll see what I can do."

"Oh, thank you." Siran said.

Flora felt her love surface for this good man, but she worried for him. He never got enough rest. Every day he walked all over the city pleading for money and food for the refugees, then at night he'd visit those in the hospital who were dying from typhus. Many feared he'd become vulnerable to the dreaded disease.

She noticed Siran's overt glances at the two men standing beside the Protestant minister.

Pointing to the handsomely dressed couple, Flora said, "Verkin will be living with Mr. and Mrs. Shar." Then her facial expression turned austere. "I'm to go with Mr. Andonian."

"When will I see you again?"

"They'll be attending church services on Sundays," the Reverend interrupted.

Flora felt distress drain away from her face. Mr. Andonian would have to bring her to church. Both her cousin and the reverend would be looking for her. Her eyes fixed on the reverend for a frightful moment. She didn't want to leave the safety of his compound. The sound in her goodbye resonated with fear. Following the Shars and Mr. Andonian outside, Flora felt the muscles in her face twitch. Not remembering when she felt worse, she watched her sister and the nice couple walk away in the opposite direction. Now separated from her entire family, she felt helpless. She was alone. Her vision blurred from tears. She could hardly see. The air grew colder. She shivered.

"Quickly," Mr. Andonian said. "My wife is waiting."

Flora clutched her Bible.

The sun dropped below the horizon. Flora watched an Arab, his *galabia* flowing behind him as he walked the street lighting the gas lights. The last time she saw gas lights casting their yellow glow was in Constantinople. The memory was bittersweet. She felt another chill and wrapped the shawl around her.

Twenty minutes later Flora observed more and more garbage strewn in the streets. They were no longer in the more affluent part of the city.

Darkness descended when they finally reached Mr. Andonian's home. His house was much like the others on the street, small and packed close together. Flora knew they were run down, even though it was too dark to see clearly.

Following Mr. Andonian through the front door, she was affronted by the smell of urine and stumbled over wet diapers on the compacted dirt floor. A kerosene lamp flickered in a corner, giving the room a gloomy cast. Silhouettes of three children, two still in diapers, sat in the opposite corner. Dirty clothes, sticks, and broken toys were scattered everywhere. The place was a mess.

The youngest child, about a year old, crawled to Flora, grasped her leg and pulled himself up. He smelled. His diaper was soaked. The other two children sat watching, their mouths open.

Recoiling, Flora knew she was not brought here for her protection.

One of the diapered children threw a stick at the younger one. He screamed.

"Stop yelling!" Rushing into the room was an older woman, a torn, patched dress hanging loosely on her large body. Her long hair was dirty and tangled. "Ahh," she said noticing the young girl. "The Reverend found someone."

Flora stared at the tall woman, knowing at once she was to be feared.

"Her name is Flora," Mr. Andonian said.

"Well, you can start now young lady. Pick up the clothes. You'll wash them tomorrow." She pointed to the two youngest. "Change their diapers. My daughter and her husband will be home soon." She turned to leave.

Flora, staring in disbelief and wondering if she was Mrs. Andonian, watched Mr. Andonian follow the contemptible woman out of the room. Now she knew for sure. She was to be a servant. Her dreams were going to be sucked dry by this detestable family and these unruly children.

The two older children started fighting. The eldest, around four years old, threw another stick at Flora. It hit her head.

Flora didn't move. She stood in anger, thinking.

The woman reappeared and shouted. "Why are you still standing there!"

Flora yelled back, "I am not your servant!"

The woman smacked Flora across her face. "You'd rather be in a convoy?"

Stunned, Flora held back tears that wanted to pour out. She covered her stinging cheek with her hand, turned away from the woman and slowly picked up the diapers.

"You are a servant," Mrs. Andonian said and stormed out.

Holding the wet diapers, Flora was dazed. She stood breathless. *What's to become of me?* Later, as Flora carried a kerosene lamp and her Bible down the stairs to the basement where she was to sleep, she felt a cold draft and gagged at the horrible stench. The space was full of droppings and broken junk—nothing like her basement in Hadjin where huge barrels were stuffed with wonderful foods. Her mouth watered thinking of the barrels of olives and cheese at her home. Mr. Andonian had given her his dinner leftovers, barely enough to feed a bird. She was hungry.

She set the lamp on the dirt floor. Noticing straw packed against one wall, she thought it could make her a bed and walked toward it. A ruffling sound startled her. Two chickens roosting on the back of a broken chair started clucking.

Relieved to see only chickens, Flora spread the straw on the floor, and wrapped herself in the blanket Mr. Andonian had given her. She thought about her parents and what had become of them. Then she had a sudden image in her mind that her mother and Nubar lay dead in the desert sands. She lay sobbing in her misery.

Feeling the cold draft again, she got up and found a hole in the mud wall. She stuck her head through and knew she could squeeze herself out, but what good would that do? Where could she go? She felt so alone and helpless. Maybe, she hoped, the Reverend would find her another home.

Sunday came and went.

Mrs. Andonian said there was no time for church.

Flora now knew this woman had more than a simple, mean streak. She was cruel.

TWENTY SIX

IS THERE ANY HOPE?

Another two Sundays passed, and Flora still hadn't been allowed to go to church. The last two weeks had been even more difficult than her first. With a constant barrage of orders, Mrs. Andonian never let Flora rest. The woman was a harsh overseer.

Trying to keep her spirits up became more difficult every day, and Flora began to worry about her own survival. The last three nights she had awakened shivering and perspiring profusely. She was unwell and had lost even more weight. The Andonians, stingy with their food, often left her hungry. They squeezed all of her energy and gave her nothing in return.

What fate had brought her here? And why the overwhelming love experience in the desert? Did it mean she was supposed to change these people by extending love to them? That would be the Christian way, but she didn't have the will or the strength to do it.

Her physical health waning, she decided she needed to escape soon. She had a plan, but had to learn Arabic before she could flee from this detestable family. Since part of her daily chores was to wash clothes in the nearby river, she cajoled young Arab girls lined by the river's edge every morning into teaching her Arabic. Daily she practiced speaking to them. Mastering the language was her passport to freedom. Turkish gendarmes left Arab children alone.

The next Sunday when Flora finished cleaning up after the family breakfast, she sneaked back down into the basement. She found a warm egg on her straw bed. She cracked it open and swallowed it whole. Then she put on her only clean dress, the one given to her by the matron of the orphanage. She climbed back up the stairs and walked through the kitchen past Mr. and Mrs. Andonian.

"Where do you think you're going, little girl!" Mrs. Andonian shouted.

"To church." Flora held her head high and marched out the front door.

Mr. Andonian sprang from his chair and flew out the door. "I'll go with you."

Flora knew the mousy little man wouldn't let her go to church alone. He'd be afraid of what she'd say to the Reverend. Besides, she needed him. She had no idea how to get to the church.

"Who's going to wash these?" Mrs. Andonian yelled, standing in the doorway holding two dirty diapers.

Flora glanced back. She wanted to laugh. The woman looked ridiculous with her mouth hanging open. Mr. Andonian bolted past his wife and quickly caught up to Flora.

"I'm sorry I didn't take you to church before today."

His apology sounded sincere, but Flora ignored him and kept right on walking. She kept a stoic face as he tried to make conversation. He told her about the central railroad station where he sometimes worked cleaning floors and that the station was located in the absolute center of the Ottoman Empire. She pretended to listen to the man as he rattled on, but she was busy attending to and memorizing the streets.

They crossed into an affluent part of the city. A home with three floors covering half the block caught Flora's attention. Its bright white color reflected pink against the morning sun. Decorative blue tiles along the edge of the roof made a colorful base for the white latticework that rose above the roof. More latticework screens surrounded the balcony on one section of the house. A dark skinned man stood by the front entrance.

"Who lives there?" Flora asked, wondering if the dark man was a eunuch.

"Oh, that's Ahmed Pasha's home. He's very rich."

"He must be to have a home that large."

"I know him," Mr. Andonian said, raising his chin.

Flora stopped. "You do?"

"Yes. I sometimes see him in the railroad station. He goes to Damascus often." He pointed to the latticed balcony. "That's his harem." A lustful smile crossed his face.

Flora noticed two girls in rose colored veils looking through the diamond shaped spaces in the latticework. Two others were on the roof looking out onto the street. Flora continued on, thinking the harem was a prison even though the ladies were clothed in fine silks.

Mr. Andonian, still gaping at the young harem girls, sighed, turned, and hurried to catch Flora.

When they arrived at the church Flora walked through the compound still crowded with tattered and scruffy refugees. She saw Verkin and rushed to her sister. They hugged. Flora didn't want to let go.

"Why haven't you come before today?" Verkin asked, releasing the embrace.

Flora stared at Mr. Andonian. His face flushed, and he stepped away from the two girls.

"God, you're pale." Verkin put her hand on Flora's forehead.

"I haven't been well."

"You look terrible."

Managing to smile, Flora said, "And you look wonderful." Verkin wore a new green dress covered with white and yellow daisies. Her hair shined. Flora longed to be as clean. She lowered her voice. "I have to find a new home. Could the Shars take me too?"

Verkin took Flora's hand, a worried look crossing her face. I'll ask them tonight. They're really nice." She smiled. "Come, let's find a seat for the service."

Flora held her sister back. "Please... ask Mr. Shar to escort us back to the Andonians today. I'm... afraid."

Verkin's eyes widened.

Flora shook her head. "No, not that. Mrs. Andonian would kill that little man if he tried anything. Please, just come. I don't want to go back there alone."

Verkin, her eyes narrowing, nodded and led Flora into the church. Finding space in a pew near the back, Flora sat so close to her sister that their hips touched.

"The Reverend gave Siran a job helping the matron," Verkin said and stretched to look for her cousin. "I see them. Siran and Krikor are up front with the orphans."

Flora saw her orphans sitting together, clean and attentive, and as she sat down she overheard a conversation from the people sitting in the next pew. Baron Hovaness had been taken to the hospital.

God, she silently prayed. *Don't let Mr. Hovaness be seriously ill. The orphanage depends upon him.* When Reverend Eskijian walked by to approach the pulpit, Flora was taken aback. His face was ashen.

After singing two hymns, it was time for his sermon. He closed his Bible and said, "Because you fed me when I was hungry and sheltered me when I needed shelter...." He paused and looked at the congregation. "We must all help." That was his sermon. The service was over. He greeted parishioners by the door. "Why haven't you come before today?" he asked Flora and reached for her hands. "You don't look well." His eyes wandered through the crowd and settled on Mr. Andonian. "Are you being treated well?"

"Please, Sir, can you find me another home?" Pleading, Flora gripped his hands.

"I'll try. Look." He grinned. "Here come your orphans."

"Hi, Flora." Six of them approached and stood behind near her.

"Hi Verkin," an eight-year-old girl said.

Flora extended her arms and little Vartan flew into them. Picking him up, she said, "You're getting heavier."

He giggled.

Flora set him down, surprised she could hold him at all. "You all look wonderful." Then she heard her cousin's voice. "Flora, are you all right?"

Siran turned to her son, Krikor. "Run. Tell the matron Flora needs medicine." She patted his rump, and he was off.

"I'd better tell Mr. Andonian that I need to see the matron." Flora turned only to see the Reverend talking to him. "On second thought, maybe he'll leave without me." The three girls zigzagged through the already crowded compound filling up with even more ragged refugees. Flora was too sick to see or recognize their pain. She stumbled, caught herself and managed to walk up the stairs leading to the orphanage.

"Flora, what's wrong?" the matron asked as she hugged the bedraggled Hadjin girl.

Flora mentioned her nightly shivers.

"Sounds like malaria," the matron said. She opened a medicine chest, wrapped seven quinine tablets in a handkerchief, and gave them to Flora. "These should help, but you also need food and rest."

"There's not much chance of that at the Andonians."

"Maybe the Pastor can find you a different home."

"He said he'd try," Flora responded.

"I can see Mr. Shar," Verkin said, glancing out the window. "We'd better go. I don't want to keep him waiting."

Waving goodbye, Flora didn't want to leave the safety and warmth of the orphanage, but she followed Verkin through the compound to the gate where Mr. Shar stood.

"You remember my sister?" Verkin asked, holding Flora's hand.

"Yes. She's staying with Mr. Andonian."

"Can we take her back to the Andonians?" Verkin asked.

"Please, Mr. Shar." Flora pleaded.

"I think that's possible." Mr. Shar placed his hand on Flora's shoulder and noticed Mr. Andonian hurrying toward them. He gazed into Flora's tired eyes. "You're so pale."

"Hello. Nice to see you again," Mr. Andonian said, extending his hand to the tall, gray-haired man.

After a brief handshake, Mr. Shar said, "We'd like to accompany you home. Verkin would like to spend more time with Flora."

Mr. Andonian hesitated. "Er... ah... why yes, of course."

They walked outside. Two horse carriages were waiting in the street for business.

Flora and Verkin followed the two men for half a block and heard Mr. Shar ask, "In which part of the city did you say you lived?"

Mr. Andonian didn't answer.

"Kalasseh," Flora said.

"Oh," Mr. Shar said. He turned toward Flora and smiled. "That's pretty far from my home." He signalled for a cab.

The open phaeton approached and stopped. They climbed in, Flora and Verkin sitting together, still holding hands. The horses pulled away.

No one talked.

Flora fixed her eyes on Mr. Andonian. He looked away, obviously uncomfortable. As they approached Kalasseh, the smells grew heavier. Flora, no longer offended by the rotting stench, noticed Mr. Shar wrinkling his nose.

"Turn down this street," Mr. Andonian said to the driver. The street was filled with unaccompanied children and dogs running through dung. Chickens and roosters dodged the horses' hoofs.

When the carriage stopped in front of Mr. Andonian's house, Flora noticed the door open, then quickly close.

Mr. Andonian jumped out, extended his hand to Flora, and said to Mr. Shar, "Thank you. I'd invite you in but my wife is not well."

"She looked fine this morning," Flora said as she stepped out of the carriage.

Mr. Shar smiled. "My wife is expecting us for lunch." He pulled a gold watch from his vest pocket. "We should have been home thirty minutes ago."

Flora grasped her sister's hand one last time before the carriage pulled away. The phaeton turned down a street and disappeared. Her heart sank.

The front door sprung opened. "Girl! Get in here. Now!"

Mr. Andonian restrained Flora with his hand. "Today is Sunday."

"What does that mean?"

"It means she needs a day off!" he shouted and escorted Flora into the house. "I'll bring you lunch, Flora… a good lunch. And another blanket."

Flora, her eyes heavy, nodded, went into the kitchen and washed down a quinine pill with water. Mr. Andonian handed her a blanket.

As she started down the stairs, the chickens ruffled their feathers. They hopped off their perch, waited, and when she reached the basement floor, they walked along with her, one on each side. Wrapping both blankets around her, Flora lay down in the straw and fell into a deep sleep. The chickens snuggled quietly next to her.

The hole in the mud wall gave the chickens access to the basement and the back yard. From outside, the rooster's boastful crow greeted the morning sun and woke Flora. Opening her eyes, she realized she had slept the entire afternoon, evening and night.

Noticing a tin box on the floor next to her, she sat up, opened it and gasped. Her eyes feasted on slices of cold lamb. Taking the thinnest slice, Flora forced herself to chew slowly, otherwise she'd feel terrible pains when her famished body received the heavier food. She chewed and chewed and chewed, savoring every bite.

Upstairs the family started to move about. It was time to go to work. She collected the eggs laid that morning and took them to the kitchen. Once in a great while one of the chickens laid an extra one— just for her. But not today.

Since that day in church five days ago, Mr. Andonian acted more kindly toward Flora. But not his wife, however. Daily she cast verbal bombardments toward the young Hadjin girl.

Flora hated the woman.

Did she dare hope that the Reverend found her a new home or that the Shar's would take and protect her?

Her night shivers having ceased and feeling somewhat stronger, Flora went to church with Mr. Andonian the following Sunday. But as they entered the crowded compound, Flora sensed something was seriously wrong. People were grieving. She rushed through the yard and left Mr. Andonian standing at the gate. She ran up the orphanage steps two at a time, opened the door and stopped. The faces of all the children were expressionless. Flora rushed to the matron. "What's wrong?"

"The Reverend was taken to the hospital. He has typhus." The matron brushed her hand against Flora's cheek. "But, at least, you look better."

"The quinine helped." Flora gripped the matron's arm. A pang of fear shot through her stomach. "Will he get well?"

The woman sighed. "We're praying."

"And Mr. Hovaness?" Flora asked. "How is he?"

Tears welled in the matron's eyes. "He died the day before yesterday."

Flora was stunned. Siran and Krikor rushed to her.

"Did you hear the bad new?" Siran asked.

Flora nodded, unable to speak.

Verkin and Mr. Shar entered the bleak room. Mr. Shar placed his hand on Flora's shoulder. "All we can do is pray." Turning toward the matron, he said, "I'd like to take the girls and Krikor home for lunch today, with your permission,

"Everything is so unsettled," the matron responded. Better not today. If they are picked up and sent out with a convoy the Reverend couldn't intervene." She walked toward the waiting children. "It's time for prayer," she said and motioned for Flora and her group to follow them into the church.

As they prayed for the Reverend's recovery, Flora felt the heavy sadness hanging in the musty air. It overwhelmed her. If the Reverend died, what will happen to all those who depended upon him, including her?

Three days later the news spread. Reverend Eskijian had joined God in his heavenly home.

TWENTY-SEVEN

IMPERIL

The last time Flora saw Verkin was a month ago, at the Reverend's funeral where hundreds of Armenians courageously gathered together to pay tribute to the man who had given his life to help those in need. Not only was her heart heavy with the Reverend's loss and the fear that gendarmes would storm the cemetery and deport them all, but it was then Flora learned she'd have to stay with the Andonians.

Mr. Shar said he couldn't take her. He was too well known in the city, especially by the police. They visited his business periodically to collect taxes, or *baksheesh.* The police already knew of Verkin. He had told them she was his wife's niece from Beirut, and if Flora came to live with them, they'd get suspicious, and maybe even deport him. Verkin never left their home without him or his wife. It was too dangerous—for the Shars as well as for Verkin.

After the Reverend's death, the orphanage found it difficult to feed the eighty orphans. Gendarmes made numerous sweeps and deported the man the Pastor's wife had hired to run the orphanage. Then they deported the second man she hired. Funds were drying up. The orphanage was faltering.

During one of the raids the gendarmes found Siran. They took her and her son away, but not very far away.

Flora saw Krikor often. He'd visit her at the Andonians and bring her food from the Shars. He told Flora that one of the gendarmes liked his mother and had offered her a job. The house where his mother worked was big and soldiers came and went all day long. But Siran had a new friend. A German officer. He wanted to find Krikor a place in the German orphanage.

Having learned Arabic, Krikor became street smart overnight. He often wandered through the city. Whenever he saw a convoy on their way to Der-el-Zor, he'd ask the refugees to find his and Flora' family when they reached their final destination. "They're from Hadjin. Please tell them we're all okay."

And he was all of six years old.

* * *

Three months passed. Aleppo was filled with Armenian refugees hiding like criminals. Once useful and important, they now thought only of survival. Half-starved, cold, sick, and avoiding detection, they'd go from house to house begging for bread.

Every morning men in two wheeled ox-carts rode through the streets. Loading the dead and covering them with lye, they took the shriveled facsimiles of what once were human beings and dumped them in a cemetery on the outskirts of the city.

It got worse. The government requisitioned all the grain and killed animals arbitrarily to feed the army. Food was scarce. Prices soared. The Andonians became desperate for money.

"Sell her," Mrs. Andonian said to her husband.

"I can't do that."

"You must."

"No!"

"You want us to starve, instead?"

"I won't be able to live with myself."

"If we don't eat, we won't live!" Mrs. Andonian stood directly in front of her husband, her nose almost touching the center of his forehead. "Sell her."

* * *

It was mid-morning. As Flora returned from the river with a basket of wet clothes, she saw Mr. Andonian. A dark brown man accompanied him.

Flora froze. Was he Ahmed Pasha's eunuch? Eunuchs and harem girls were synonymous. No, she thought, it's unthinkable. Mr. Andonian wouldn't... couldn't, sell her. Her blood ran cold.

When Mr. Andonian saw her, he looked the other way. The dark man followed him into the house. The door closed.

Apprehensive, Flora went to the back where she normally hung the wet clothes. She carried the full basket inside and dropped it on the kitchen floor. Determined to know, she marched into the living room. Mr. Andonian and the eunuch were the only two in the house. Where were the children? Everyone was gone.

"Flora," Mr. Andonian said and stopped. "Flora," he said again, hesitated, and then pointed to the eunuch. "He's taking you to Ahmed Pasha."

Flora narrowed her eyes and stared at Mr. Andonian. "What right do you have to sell me!"

Mr. Andonian couldn't respond.

"I have to get my things." Flora turned and marched toward the stairs. She turned again and looked directly into Mr. Andonian's eyes. "May God have mercy on your soul." She flew down the stairs, grabbed her Bible, got on her hands and knees, and squeezed herself through the hole the chickens used to go into the back yard. Once outside, the two chickens and the rooster ruffled their feathers and walked toward her. Flora ran out into the street only to see Mrs. Andonian waiting, as if she had expected Flora to do what she did.

"Where do you think you're going, little girl!"

Flora rushed by her and felt the ringing sting as Mrs. Andonian whacked her across her head.

Dazed, she fell to the ground.

Mr. Andonian and the eunuch came out of the house.

"I'll take her now," the eunuch said in his high pitched voice. He reached down and picked her up.

Flora brushed the dirt off her arms. Her nostrils flared as she stared at the cruel woman. Hatred poured through her eyes. She turned and walked alongside the dark man. When the Andonian home was no longer in sight, Flora bolted, but she was no match for the eunuch. Within seconds he caught her and yanked her toward him.

"I'm sorry to do this," he said. Taking rope from his pocket, he tied her wrist to his.

Flora struggled to free herself, but the rope cut into her flesh. Blood seeped out and as she watched it slide down her arm, her mind was racing. How was she going to get out of this? Then she saw Krikor.

Her young cousin's eyes bulged when he saw her.

"He's taking me to Ahmed Pasha," Flora yelled.

The young boy gasped and ran in the direction of the Shars.

Flora arrived at Ahmed Pasha's opulent home and was greeted by gentle sounds of water trickling in a fountain in the front courtyard. Taken to the side of the house, Flora noticed stairs leading up to the roof. Near the stairwell was a door.

The eunuch took her down the side path to the door and knocked. A dark skinned teenage girl wearing only a tan chiffon skirt and a gold braided belt wrapped around her waist opened the door. Flora assumed she was a slave.

About eighteen, the girl extended her hand, brought Flora into the harem and closed the door. She stripped Flora naked and pointed to a shallow blue tiled pool. Steam moved across the surface of the water. Splotches of water and wet footprints were on the floor. Wondering who else had been in this bathing area, Flora didn't hesitate. She jumped in and splashed the warm heavenly water all over her face. The slave girl handed her a bar of soap, and Flora rubbed it over her dirty body. The soap was soft, had the scent of roses, and formed bubbles all over her skin. She kept passing the bubbly bar under her nose enjoying its fragrance. She wanted to scrub away the putrid smells of the Andonians.

The black girl reached for Flora's hand and took Ahmed Pasha's newest possession through a door into a larger room. Billows of steam hit Flora in the face. The dark girl gave her a gentle push and closed the door. Not seeing anyone in the misty room, she sat on the cement bench and leaned back against the damp tiled wall, closed her eyes, stuck her tongue out to taste the steamy vapors enveloping her and wondered how long it would take to loosen the dirt embedded in her skin. Flora let her mind drift back to Hadjin when she, Verkin, her mother and grandmother would take their weekly trek to the Turkish bath. It was such a happy, social event. The girls and women would sit nude in the steam bath, talk about the town's events and gossip about the townspeople. It had been more than six months since Flora had been in a bath.

The slave girl returned, took her back into the room with the pool and gave her another bar of soap. Flora lovingly inhaled its orange fragrance. She jumped into the warm water and scrubbed away. Savoring this piece of joy, Flora refused to think beyond the moment.

Holding a large, white towel the slave girl stood by the pool. When Flora walked up the steps, the dark girl wrapped the heavy towel around Flora's little body, took her into a room where another bare breasted slave girl was standing by a massage table. Climbing up onto the table, Flora handed the towel to the girl, stretched out and lay on her stomach. The dark girl's hands and fingers felt gentle as she rubbed Flora's back and legs with oil that smelled of almonds. Flora drifted into a light sleep and barely heard the girl say, "Turn over."

"Please. Turn over."

She felt the girl's hand slip under her shoulder and give a quick flip. Flora found herself lying on her back, fully relaxed. She closed her eyes again and drifted into fond memories of the Hadjin bathhouse.

Sometime later she heard a mature woman's voice. "I'm ready for her."

Flora felt an arm slide under her back and lift her into a sitting position. Opening her eyes, Flora saw an elegant black woman wearing a long, flowing blue linen robe and a blue and white striped turban.

"Come, little one," the woman said and extended her hand. "I will make you beautiful."

Suddenly Flora realized why she was being pampered. The bubble of pleasure burst. With trepidation, she climbed down off the table and followed the woman into yet another room. On the floor were bolts of fabrics. A sewing machine sat in the middle of the room.

The woman reached for one of the fabrics and said, "I will make you a lovely gown. This is a special evening."

Oh God, Flora thought. She means tonight. Her heart raced.

Holding the edge of the flowery yellow silk material against Flora's face, she said, "No, this color is not for you." The woman picked up another bolt of fabric. "Green should be better." She held the fine

Indian silk under Flora's eyes. "Yes. It brings out the green in your eyes." Letting the bolt drop to the floor, she draped the delicate fabric around Flora, her hand following and caressing the curves of Flora's body. She pinched Flora's breast and smiled as Flora backed away. "Not much there." Letting the material drop to the floor, she reached for a plain, simple black cotton dress and handed it to Flora. "Put this on for now."

Welcoming anything to cover her chilled, naked body, Flora threw on the dress. Not given underwear, she wondered if she was not supposed to wear underwear in the harem. Uncomfortable and embarrassed, she folded the sides of the dress in front of her thighs.

"Come. I will take you to meet the other girls."

Flora followed the woman up a stairway that opened onto an area that looked more like a playroom than a roof. Five pretty girls around her sister's age were playing cards. Their veils sat on the floor beside them.

When they saw Flora they giggled. "Oh, my, Ahmed Pasha is going to love you," one of them said. "He likes his girls little!" They laughed even louder.

"I'll come back for you later." The elegant dark woman turned and left.

Looking at the five girls, Flora stood frozen.

Bare-footed, the bracelets around their ankles jingling, the girls approached Flora. Their colorful chiffon skirts flowed around their moving legs. All five had the same tattoo etched into their foreheads.

"I'm Tamar," one of them said. She was pregnant.

"You're Armenian?"

Tamar smiled. "Yes." She introduced Flora to the girls. Two were Arabs and the other two were Kurds. The girls gathered around Flora and tried to make her feel comfortable. They told her that Ahmed Pasha also had four wives, seven sons and three daughters.

Tamar told Flora she had come from the city of Diarbekir in Turkey. She had been separated from her mother and sisters when a gendarme stole her, raped her and sold her to a Kurd. The Kurd then sold her to Ahmed Pasha. "I'd rather be here than in a convoy," she said. Tears welled in her eyes and she began to sob. "I miss my mother."

Flora put her arm around Tamar. "I miss mine too." Beyond tears, she tried not to think of her family. It was too painful.

The eyes of the other four girls poured sympathetic understanding toward the two Armenian girls. Flora wondered about their backgrounds and how they came into Ahmed Pasha's life.

"Come," one of the girls said. "See what's in our trunk!"

The old, black trunk, its brass hinges scratched, rested at the far end of the roof. A waxed canvass cover lay on the floor beside it. Flora followed the girls and watched as the young Arab girl pulled out some of the items—embroidery, needle point, trinkets, playing cards and a well-worn Bible.

"That's mine," Flora said taking the Holy Book and opening the cover to Miss Webb's father's inscription. "How did it get here?"

"One of the servants put it there," the Arab girl said.

"Ohh." Flora had been so engrossed in her bath, she had forgotten about the Holy Book. Happy to have it back, she carefully placed it into the trunk and became interested in something else—the stairs she had seen earlier.

"Where do the stairs go?" she asked.

"Into our private garden," Tamar said.

"Hmmm." Flora looked down the narrow steps and wondered. Could she escape? It looked too easy.

The Arab girl threw everything back into the trunk. "Let's tell Flora all about Ahmed Pasha." Her hands flew to her mouth, and she giggled.

Sitting Flora down, the girls explained in detail how Ahmed Pasha liked his concubines. Sometimes the girls had to play with him for a long time before he was up and ready. He was getting old. The more the girls talked and laughed, the more Flora cringed. She was going to lose her virginity tonight. And to a Turk. But wasn't this place better than at the Andonians? She loved the pampering and there would be plenty to eat, but Ahmed Pasha could get rid of her anytime he felt like it. Then what would the rest of her life be like? No Armenian would ever marry her.

She looked again at the stairs. Maybe....

TWENTY EIGHT

AN ANXIOUS SISTER

Breathless, Krikor ran up the stairs to the Shars' home and banged on the door. "Verkin!" he shouted. The door opened. Verkin immediately saw the fear in her young cousin's face. "What's wrong?"

"Flora!" Krikor slapped his hand against his chest and gasped. "The darkie took her to Ahmed Pasha!"

"What?" Pulling her little cousin inside, Verkin closed the door and knelt to be level with his eyes. "Are you sure?"

"I saw them together… ah… ah… The darkie and Flora together." He bent his head and gazed at the floor. "There was nothing I could do."

"No!" Verkin knew of Ahmed Pasha. He was rich, rich, rich. She paced the room not knowing what to do. The Shars weren't home, and she was afraid to leave the house. What if the gendarmes picked her up? "Do you know where Ahmed Pasha lives?" she asked Krikor.

The youngster nodded, his eyes widening.

Verkin increased her pace, her face creased with worry. Walking into her bedroom she opened her armoire and spied the black dress pushed to the back. She pulled out the crumpled dress and held it up. A black *charshaf* inside the dress fell to the floor. She picked it up. Lucky, she hadn't thrown away the dress. She dashed into the kitchen, grabbed the iron on the table, stirred the hot coals in the stove, and set the iron to heat.

Krikor sat at the kitchen table. Chewing his fingernail, he watched Verkin iron the dress.

She held it up. "It looks fine." Verkin left the room and returned wearing the black *chador*.

"Why are you wearing that dress?"

"I have to look like a Moslem."

"Oh," he said. "You'd better cover your face."

Verkin removed the barrette from behind her head and let her hair fall down to her shoulders. She wrapped the *charshaf* around her head.

"That's better," the youngster said.

Verkin pulled the *charshaf* off and slumped into a chair. "I don't know." Leaving the safety of the Shars' home made her nervous.

"You're not going to leave her there, are you?"

"I have to wait till the Shars come home."

An hour later Verkin explained to the Shars what had happened. They felt bad, but said they couldn't help. Ahmed Pasha now owned Flora, and Mr. Shar, a Christian, didn't dare interfere with Moslem customs. Verkin knew that gendarmes constantly threatened Mr. Shar, but *baksheesh* always placated those threats. Now Mr. Shar told her that he was afraid the government would requisition his wholesale food business, if he were even suspected of stealing a girl from Ahmed Pasha's harem.

Verkin had to do it alone. And if she was caught, she couldn't admit she knew the Shars.

"You can always say you work with my mother in the big house," Krikor piped up.

Repulsed at the thought, Verkin wondered how much her street-smart six-year-old cousin understood about the "house" in which his mother worked. She brushed the top of his head, realizing his idea was probably a good one.

Walking to the French doors by the balcony, Verkin pulled back the lace curtains and watched carriages drive by. Horses' hooves made soft sounds on the unpaved road. A lone man dressed in a *galabia* and carrying bundles walked along the side of the quiet road. Verkin closed the curtains and took Krikor's hand. "We'll wait till it gets dark." Perspiration dripped from her forehead, stinging her eyes.

Later, when Verkin stepped out onto the balcony, the gaslights along the street were lit. Time to go. Stepping back inside, she slipped the charshaf over her head and face. She went to Mrs. Shar and hugged her.

"Please be careful." Tears welled in Mrs. Shar's eyes. "We love you, Verkin. Remember that." She handed Verkin a black shawl. "You'll need this for Flora."

"We're anxious for your return." Mr. Shar said.

Verkin nodded goodbye, her eyes betraying certainty. She grasped Krikor's hand. They slipped out the front door, ran down the stairs and looked up at the balcony. The Shars stood behind the lace curtains, watching.

Krikor and Verkin ran. After crossing two streets, they heard men's voices and saw soldiers. Krikor pulled Verkin into an alley. It was pitch black. They leaned against the back of a house, waiting, holding hands and breaths.

Slurred voices grew louder. Were they singing? Minutes later the voices faded. Verkin and Krikor walked gingerly toward the street. Krikor saw four men staggering and pushing one another. Three were soldiers. He extended his hand to Verkin. She took it. Just as they entered the street, one of the soldiers turned. "You!" he yelled, slipped and fell.

Another soldier bent to pick him up and saw Verkin. "Little lady, come here," he called and hiccuped. He stood, staggered, lost his balance and fell against the street light.

Verkin stared at the huge facial birthmark. It was Alai. "No!" She bolted and ran.

Krikor chased her and heard one of the men yell, "Don't bother Moslem women. I don't want trouble from the police."

The two runaways continued to race through the quiet streets. For four long blocks all they saw were lights reflecting from windows in the fine two storey homes. A carriage pulled up in front of one of the nice houses, a man stepped out, paid the driver and looked with surprise at the speeding boy and girl.

"I know that soldier," Verkin said, feeling safe enough to slow down to a fast walk. "He's been after me since I left Hadjin."

"What?"

"I'll explain later," she blurted as sounds from horses pounding against the compacted dirt road unnerved her. More soldiers! She flew around the corner and fled into a dark lane, Krikor right on her heels. Her heart beating faster than she could breathe, she pressed her hand against her mouth. Her knees shook. As the sounds of hooves faded into the distance, she relaxed and could no longer hear the drum-like rhythms from her heart.

"We should go," Krikor said and cautiously walked toward the well-lighted street. "Come. It's clear!"

Her knees still shaking, Verkin followed her young cousin. She told herself she had to get a grip on herself if she was to save her sister, but when they neared Ahmed Pasha's imposing home, she felt intense fear rise again. "How will I find her?

Krikor pointed to the balcony. "Up there, behind the screens."

"There are screens on the roof, too," Verkin said. Quietly they walked ahead, their eyes searching the huge estate.

"Wait here," Krikor said. Running past the house, he waved to the dark-skinned man standing by what had to be the front entrance to the harem. The eunuch wore a red turban, a fluffy white satin shirt, black pantaloons, and a wide red sash around his waist. Krikor ran back, waved again, touched his forehead and extended his hand. "Salaam," he shouted to the eunuch.

With a high-pitched voice, the dark man yelled, "Go away."

Krikor rushed back to where Verkin stood just out of sight. "I saw girls on the roof. And there are stairs on the side of the house that go up there."

"Won't he see me?"

"Not if I distract him." Krikor paused. He, too, looked scared. "Are you ready?"

Verkin nodded. She wiped her clammy palms against her dress. As Krikor approached the guard, Verkin felt her hands become damp again. She watched her cousin kneel down to the ground in an elaborate Moslem prayer position. The eunuch burst into laughter, and she cautiously walked toward them. When the dark man bent down and lifted Krikor to his feet, she sped down the side of the house. When she reached the stairs, her heart again sounded as if drums were beating wildly. She grasped the wrought-iron railing and inched up the narrow stairs. Her under arms wet, she felt perspiration slide down her side. Just a little more, she told herself. Six more steps and she'd be at the top. Her knees wobbled. She held the rail tightly, turned her head and caught a glimpse of the lights spreading across the city. Smothering a gasp, she dared not enjoy the wondrous sight. Seeing so many electric lights was staggering. Hadjin was never like this. Perspiration dripped into her eyes and brought her back to the here and now. Close to the top, she edged up and peered over.

Flora sat in a circle with five other girls. Empty plates of food lay inside the circle.

She ducked. Now, what? Terror seized her. What if she was caught? What terrible things would they do to her? She wanted to run away. Her vision blurred. She wiped her wet eyes with her sleeve. Finally, she mustered enough nerve to look again. She inched-up another two stairs, stood quietly and waited.

Fortunately, Flora and only one other girl faced her. Seeing the startled expression on her sister's face, Verkin knew Flora had seen her. Her breath quickened. She sneaked back down the two stairs and waited.

"Oh, my God," Flora murmured. Stunned, she sat staring at the stairs.

"What?" Tamar asked, turning toward Flora.

Flora sat impassively, not knowing what to do.

Tamar scooted so close to Flora their hips touched. "It'll be over soon."

Flora didn't react. She merely placed her hand on Tamar's thigh, as though she was saying she needed help.

"She's scared," the Arab girl said and laughed so hard she fell on her side. Rolling over on to her hands and knees, she slowly crept toward Flora. "Tonight you belong to Ahmed Pasha." She lunged at Flora. "Ahh!"

Flora found herself lying on her back, the Arab girl bouncing on top of her.

Tamar pushed her off Flora. "Weren't you the first time?" Tamar retorted, lifted her Armenian friend and embraced a startled Flora.

Flora tightened the embrace and whispered, "My sister's here."

Tamar braced her head against Flora and then stood. "Let's see if Flora's gown is finished." She walked toward the inside stairs. Two of the girls followed her.

The Arab girl didn't. "I'll stay with Flora," she said.

"No," Tamar said. "Flora needs to be alone for a while. She needs to think about her big night with Ahmed Pasha."

"He's a pig," the Arab girl said. "Think about that. And tomorrow you, too, will be wearing his tattoo." She licked two of her fingers and rubbed her forehead as if she were trying to wipe away the mark that told the world she belonged to Ahmed Pasha. A tear fell down her cheek as she followed the girls down the stairs.

Flora jumped up, ran to the trunk, pulled out her Bible, and followed Verkin who had already rushed down the steps. Both were breathing hard when they reached the bottom. Krikor was there, waiting. They followed him to the corner of the house. "Wait." He picked up a handful of pebbles and walked gingerly toward the front entrance. "Hey," he yelled and pitched the small stones at the eunuch.

The startled man blocked his face as the stones hit his chest. "You!" he yelled to Krikor, who was already half way up the block. "I'll get you!" The eunuch flew after the youngster.

"Now!" Grasping Flora's hand, Verkin ran in the opposite direction. They took cover in the first dark alley they crossed. "Cover your head." Verkin said, giving Flora the shawl. Hovering in the darkness for what seemed for more than an hour, Verkin gathered enough nerve to sneak toward the street. A carriage passed by. No one was in sight. She motioned for Flora to come. They walked toward the Shar's home, trying to appear unruffled. When they turned into the next street, Krikor stood under a gas light, waiting.

"Hi Flora," he said, as if nothing unusual had happened. "When did you become a Moslem?"

The smile on his face told Flora her young cousin was far older than his six years.

TWENTY NINE

A DEEPENING TRUST

That night Mrs. Shar gave Flora a folding mattress and left the two girls together in Verkin's room. Flora placed the mattress on the floor next to Verkin, grateful to be alone with her sister. She snuggled up to Verkin as they lay together. Their bodies touched. After four months of being alone, Flora needed security of family, but she didn't feel like talking. What had happened to her wonderful life? She had had such great dreams. Lying there, in this strange land, she wondered if she could ever overcome all that had happened to her. Relieved from what she perceived would have been an agonizing experience with Ahmed Pasha, she was thankful to be next to her sister instead of a smelly old Turk. But she was still too scared to sleep. She needed her mother and father. Her eyes moistened.

She was only one of the thousands of young Armenian girls separated from their families. But thank God for Tamar. Flora wondered how Tamar's mother, if she survived, would begin to look for her daughter. Tamar had been in Kurdish territory when she was stolen, and Flora's life had almost followed that of Tamar's. And the war was not yet over. What if a Turkish soldier whisked her away from Aleppo? How would her father find her? She shivered.

"Want another blanket?" Verkin asked.

"No." She rested her head against her sister's shoulder. Her nightmare of becoming orphaned surfaced, and she put her arm around Verkin. "If you weren't here...."

Verkin, a worried look on her face, said, "I saw Alai tonight."

Flora bolted to a sitting position. "Here, in Aleppo?"

Verkin nodded.

Dread filled Flora.

"I'm sure he didn't know it was me he saw."

Flora felt her throat tightening. "Was he alone?"

"No. Three of the four were soldiers."

The waiter. Flora knew the waiter had to have been one of them. Should she warn Verkin about the white slave trade? But that would frighten Verkin even more.

"We have to be careful, Flora. We can't leave the house without Mr. or Mrs. Shar."

Flora agreed. But she knew she'd not be able to stay in the Shar's home for long. Would there ever be a time when she'd feel safe again? She reached for her Bible, wanting to touch it. Miss Webb's words drifted through her mind. Hold onto hope. But maybe she was just lucky to still be alive.

The next morning Flora opened the doors to the balcony and stepped outside. She breathed in the clean air, relieved not to have the decaying smells of the Andonian neighborhood. The houses in this neighborhood were built with attractive white stone, had two or more storeys and at least one balcony. Only one home had latticework covering its curved windows. Flora assumed it was a Moslem home where the women could look out without being seen.

Krikor was walking toward the house. He was not his usual scrappy self. Something was wrong. She saw a sad-faced little boy. Flora ran to the front door and opened it.

He gave her a weak smile and walked straight into the kitchen. "Any bread? And olives?" he asked Mrs. Shar.

Mrs. Shar opened the ice chest and put a jar of black olives and a dish of feta cheese on the table. "Want some warm milk?"

He nodded.

"What's wrong?" Flora and Verkin said simultaneously. He lowered his head. "I have to go to the German orphanage."

Flora patted his back. "That's not so bad, is it?"

He took the glass of warm milk from Mrs. Shar. "I'm not an orphan. I have a mother." His eyes were teary.

"When?" Verkin asked.

"Soon." He took a sip of the milk and licked his upper lip. "My mother is moving into a house with her German friend." His eyes fell on Flora. "She says you can have her job, if you want."

Shocked, Flora reached for Verkin's arm. Why would Siran think she'd be interested in working in such a place? Did she think that Ahmed Pasha had deflowered her? "Tell your mother I'm not interested," Flora cried and marched out of the room.

A perplexed Krikor looked at Verkin. "What's wrong with her?"

"She's still scared," Verkin replied and ran after her sister.

"Flora," Mrs. Shar called out. "Don't worry. My husband will find you a good home."

* * *

Later that day when Mr. Shar returned from work, he told Flora about Plato Sawaides, a Greek national who was married to a Syrian lady. They had two young daughters and wanted Flora to help care for the children.

"He's the vice-consul of agriculture at the Greek consulate in Aleppo," Mr. Shar said to Flora, "and nothing like Mr. Andonian."

Flora didn't respond.

"I promise you, he'll treat you well. He's a very nice man."

"Is a vice-consul like an ambassador?" Flora asked.

"No," Mr. Shar responded. "The Greek ambassador is at the embassy in Constantinople."

"Oh," Flora said. "I met the American ambassador in Constantinople. My teacher Miss Webb took me to one of his embassy parties." She smiled remembering how kind the ambassador had been to her. "Can I meet him first?"

"Of course. Tomorrow. He'll come by in the afternoon."

"Thank you, Mr. Shar," Flora said, thinking about the well-bred Ambassador Morgenthau. Maybe the Greek diplomat would be just as nice.

That night as Flora fell asleep, she thought about Miss Webb and tried to hold onto hope.

THIRTY

THE DIPLOMAT

The next afternoon Flora waited with Verkin behind the lace curtains and watched a carriage pull up. Mr. Shar and another man stepped out and both men walked up the stairs to the front door.

Flora noticed that the man with Mr. Shar didn't have Greek features. Greeks, like Armenians, had olive skin and dark hair. This man was fair. He had light brown hair and the color of his eyes blended with his gray suit. He wore the same small round glasses that Ambassador Morgenthau had, but with an addition. A gold chain was attached to the glasses, and it draped behind his right ear and lay softly under his lapel.

Verkin touched her sister's shoulder. "He looks rich." But Flora saw something else. He looked like an educated man.

Mr. Shar brought the gentleman into the living room, introduced the Greek diplomat, Plato Sawaides, and extended his arm to one of the French chairs. Flora observed the man sit into the delicate chair, as if he was paying homage to the maker of the finely crafted chair. His eyes were gentle, like those of the Reverend. He was not a big man, but he projected a certain confidence. She liked him.

Mr. Sawaides' smile put Flora at ease. "What's this I hear?" he asked. "You know the American ambassador?"

"Yes. Last summer I was in Constantinople."

Mr. Sawaides leaned toward the young girl. "And...?"

"Miss Webb, my American teacher at the Hadjin mission, made it possible for me to attend Constantinople College for Girls last summer."

"How wonderful."

"Yes, and she took me to a celebration at the embassy by the Bosporus where I saw wonderful fireworks for America's independence day." Flora was nervous. "Then, later that night, we shot fireworks from a boat. It was a wonderful day."

Mrs. Shar came in the room holding a silver tray with two coffees. She presented a coffee to the Greek consul. "I hope you like it sweet."

Plato Sawaides nodded and took one of the gold leafed demitasses.

Mrs. Shar gave the second cup to her husband and quietly left the room.

"I've never met the American ambassador," Plato said to Flora, "but I'm in constant contact with Mr. Jackson, his consul-general here in Aleppo. We're doing all we can to help the Armenians who pass through the city. Ambassador Morgenthau sends money so we can buy food for them."

Flora wondered if some of the American money found its way to the Reverend's orphanage.

"But the situation worsens by the day," he continued. "What we give is only a drop of water when we need a whole ocean."

Flora didn't want to hear anymore. Images of two wheeled ox-carts picking up dead bodies every morning were too painful.

"Sir," she began and stopped. "Should I call you Mr. Sawaides?"

"Mr. Plato... everyone calls me Mr. Plato."

Flora smiled, thinking of the famous philosopher. Could the Greek's name be a good omen for her? "Sir... I mean Mr. Plato...." She smiled again and leaned forward. "Do you think the American ambassador can find out about my family? And where they are?"

Verkin scooted to the edge of her chair. "Please, Mr. Sawaides... ah... Mr. Plato."

"I will ask." Mr. Plato's face reflected compassion.

Flora felt the man was truly sympathetic. She relaxed. "Mr. Shar says you have two daughters."

"Yes." Mr. Plato smiled. "One is brand new and the other is two. And my wife needs help caring for them. Would you be agreeable to helping us?"

"Yes," Flora responded. She felt she'd be safe with the Greek diplomat. "Mr. Plato, will I be able to visit my sister?"

"Of course."

Mr. Shar gave Flora an approving nod.

A smile crossing her face, Flora stood. "I'll only be a moment." She went into Verkin's room and came out carrying Miss Webb's Bible. "I'm ready."

When Mr. Plato and Flora settled into the soft, black leather seats of the waiting carriage, they talked about their lives. Plato Sawaides's father was consul general of Aleppo's Greek consulate, and Flora understood that his family was highly respected. Diplomats carried great prestige and power not only in the Ottoman Empire but also throughout the world. The more Mr. Plato talked, the more Flora sensed a kind quality in the man. He reminded her of her own father.

Passing the moat that once protected the ancient ruins where turrets and towers still soared up into the sky, she said, "No one has told me what that is." The formidable ruins stood high on the only hill in the city.

"It's an old fortress. I'll take you there sometime. Would you like that?"

Flora nodded, but her heart grew heavy. The fortress was a remnant of old wars, and this current war had done such horrible things. Sadness constantly hung in the air of this sprawling city. Everywhere open spaces were filled with emaciated women and children lying quietly waiting to be herded like sheep to the desert interior—or just waiting to die. Aleppo was rife with heartbreaking scenes.

"I have to stop at the consulate before we go home," Mr. Plato said.

A few minutes later Flora noticed German flags waving on the steps of a large home. "Is the German orphanage nearby?" Brave, little Krikor would soon be joining her Hadjin orphans who were already living there.

"It's around the corner." The carriage turned down the street. "There." Mr. Plato pointed to a two story building.

Flora saw a young man holding the hands of two small-frightened looking children at the front entrance of the orphanage. A lady opened the door, shook her head and immediately closed the door. The man ran away, leaving the two children sobbing and standing by the closed door. Then the door opened and the two children were pulled inside. Flora's eyes welled. At least two more would be saved.

As the carriage turned into the business section of the city, she noticed two chained men shuffling along. With bent heads and stooped shoulders, the prisoners looked like old men. But something about them was familiar. She gasped. "It's Zohrab and Vartkes." She had met the two famous Armenian Parliamentarians when they were in Hadjin to dedicate the new library.

"I heard they'd been arrested," Plato said.

Flora couldn't take her eyes off the two men. They no longer projected the image of glorious, larger than life heroes who had impressed her that long ago day in Hadjin. They had aged dramatically. Zohrab's hair was now completely white.

"They are to go on trial," Plato said. "In Diarbekir."

"Why?" Flora asked, not able to comprehend why the Armenian politicians would be treated like common criminals.

"Sedition."

"What's that?"

"The Turks claim they've caused discontent against the government."

"Discontent?" Flora mumbled, not understanding. The Turks had taken her own father and now they were taking the fathers of Armenia.

Her eyes welled again.

THIRTY ONE

DANGER IN THE COVERED BAZAAR

Three months later:

The contrast in the two households' fate presented to Flora boggled her mind. Mr. Plato and his wife treated her like family, but being with them was also bittersweet. It was a constant reminder of her own happy family back home in Hadjin, and how dearly she wanted to be with them. Be that as it may, she had to wait, and until that time comes, she'd show her gratitude by fulfilling her responsibilities dutifully. She took great care in tending to the Sawaides' two children.

Hearing a knock on the door she shared with the family cook, she opened the door to see Mr. Plato and his wife standing together hand in hand. "I wanted to see you in your new blouse and skirt," Mrs. Sawaides said.

A smile spread across Flora's face. Mr. Plato's wife had given Flora a white blouse and blue plaid skirt the night before. "Thank you, Mrs. Sawaides. It's an outfit my sister would wear," Flora chuckled. "When she sees it, she'll want one just like it." Touching the sides of the skirt, Flora loved the feel of the fine cotton fabric. She was grateful at fourteen to look and feel like an ordinary young girl rather than an orphan who had to scrounge for any old rag to cover her body.

Mrs. Sawaides brushed Flora's cheek with affection. "Have a good morning. I'll have the children ready when you return."

Flora nodded, closed the door behind her and waved good-by to Mrs. Sawaides. Every morning Flora and Mr. Plato walked into town to buy the day's groceries. It was Flora's favorite part of the day, because she had the wonderful man all to herself. They'd converse in Turkish and Arabic, but mostly Turkish because he wanted to sharpen his knowledge of the language. After shopping, Mr. Plato would send Flora home with the grocery bundles, and he went to work. But she was never really comfortable without him by her side. Even though she spoke Arabic fluently and looked like any other Arab girl on the street, there was always the fear that a gendarme would stop her and find out she was Armenian and not Arab. But the city had become somewhat sane. Tattered Armenians looking like walking skeletons were no longer seen nor were the chilling oxcarts that carried the dead bodies found on Aleppo streets every morning. The exiled Armenians who had not perished were already in the unfriendly desert at Der-el-Zor.

Walking together toward the center of the city, Mr. Plato greeted men dressed in smart European suits and tipped his hat to others riding in horse carriages. Occasionally an automobile motored on the wide-paved streets in this affluent section of Aleppo. The streets burgeoned with life. Servants swept porches, stairs, and paved sidewalks in front of large wood-framed homes, and nursemaids strolled infants in baby carriages to the nearby park. Taking the two Sawaides children to the park was a bright part of Flora's afternoon duties. The vibrant greenery of the park was in direct contrast to the bland sand colored city. She loved bracing her back against the sycamore tree whose branches formed an umbrella of shade over her as she watched the children play. But before she went home today she wanted to stop at the German orphanage. "Mr. Plato, can I visit the Hadjin orphans and my cousin, Krikor, before I go home today?"

"Of course. It's good you see them occasionally."

Flora knew he'd say yes. He sensed how important it was for her to keep contact with her Hadjin roots. He was also good about letting her visit her sister every week.

"The cook needs herbs and spices," he said. "Why don't we go to the bazaar?"

Flora nodded. She loved the smells of perfume and herbs tucked in the dark corners of the city's covered bazaar, but it was also a little scary. The narrow compacted dirt passageways, the crowds of mostly Arab men and the low ceiling spotted with soot sometimes gave Flora a feeling of being smothered.

Jammed with shops and stalls, you could buy almost anything in the narrow labyrinth whose corridors teamed with life. The bazaar had become a popular trading center to accommodate the legion of camel caravans traveling to and from India. Flora loved to watch sellers and buyers haggle over prices. She never did get to go to the bazaar in Constantinople. That one was world renown.

As they passed beneath one of the arches leading into the bazaar, Flora reached for Mr. Plato's hand, not wanting to lose him. The twisting passageways were confusing. A barking dog nipped at a street cat who twisted free and sped into the crowded area. Flora raised her foot as the cat scooted by. She noticed an Arab dressed in an inexpensive *galabia* struggling with three mules tied together. He yanked the rope, and as they hurried by, the mules threw up a haze of dust in front of Flora. Smelling dung, she stepped aside.

A young boy chasing after three cackling chickens slid on the animal droppings. Falling to one knee, he rose quickly and continued to run after the chickens.

She laughed at the silly scene. Merging into the crowded corridor, Flora gripped Mr. Plato's hand more tightly. They threaded their way through two long passageways. Rays of light filtered through the open archway and cracks in the ceiling. Traces of brewed coffee filtered along the corridors as potential buyers drank from demitasses offered by fast talking hawkers. Her eyes delighted with the visual scenes. Huge burlap sacks brimming with spices and herbs lined several small stalls. Other shops and stalls sold perfumes, Persian rugs, fabrics, mostly wool, cotton and silk, gold, especially coins and jewelry, hand carved woods with inlaid ivory, mostly backgammon boards and small tables, hand made items from copper, such as Turkish coffee pots and trays, and the agents of money, the money changers who kept abreast of the many foreign currencies and their value. She knew no one was trading the English pound anymore. It was practically worthless in Aleppo.

"Ah, my favorite spice stall," Mr. Plato said and waited until a merchant from Damascus finalized an order with the owner.

Flora wanted to run her hands through the sacks lining the front of the stall. Filled with the Old World spices of zahtar, sumac, fenugreek, mahleeb, chaiman, rahan, and kimion, she wanted to take a handful of each to hold under her nose. Instead, she stood in front of the sacks and sniffed in the aromatic smells. Listening to Mr. Plato negotiate a price for his order, she smelled perfume floating through the musty air. Her nose followed the scent. She glanced at the perfume stall by the opened door leading into the courtyard of one of Aleppo's most popular mosques. Expecting to enjoy another fragrant whiff, she instead held her breath. Threatening eyes from a soldier had fixed on her. She stiffened. His birthmark told her who he was. It was Alai Oghlou.

Struggling to breathe, Flora broke into a sweat. She also recognized the man with him.

Alai rushed toward her.

Flora panicked. She moaned and squeezed Mr. Plato's hand.

"What's wrong, Flora?" Mr. Plato turned and saw Alai standing and staring at Flora. "What do you want, soldier?"

Alai didn't answer, his eyes still fixed on Flora.

Slipping his arm around Flora, Mr. Plato cradled her so their bodies touched. "You're bothering my daughter."

Alai grinned, as if he didn't believe the man. "Let me see your papers."

"We've no time for this." The man standing alongside Alai pulled at the soldier's sleeve. "Let's go."

"Not yet." Alai twisted his arm free and thrust his hand toward Mr. Plato. "Your papers!"

The Greek stepped back, reached inside his jacket to his vest pocket, pulled out his passport and opened it to the page where his diplomatic seal loomed.

"Merde!" the other man exclaimed.

"Indeed," Mr. Plato answered dryly. "And be sure to read the letter inside."

Alai snatched the passport, took out the folded letter, and read it. Blood drained from his face. His birthmark turned crimson. He refolded the letter, returned it and the passport, and quickly backed away.

His companion ran after him. "You fool," he yelled as they disappeared into the crowd.

Flora felt her knees shaking.

"Who are they, Flora?"

She burst into tears.

Plato bent down. "Who are they?" He took out a handkerchief and wiped the tears that had spilled down her cheeks.

"Demons," she managed to say.

"Mr. Sawaides, bring the girl inside," the owner of the spice stall said as he pushed aside a huge spice sack so the pair could join him inside. He pointed to a rickety folding chair where Flora could sit and poured water into a small glass. "Give her this."

Mr. Plato handed the water to Flora.

She couldn't swallow.

Mr. Plato took the glass and with his hand brushed some of the water around her lips. "I won't let anything happen to you. Now, tell me." He handed his handkerchief to her.

Flora blew her nose and with a loud sniff said, "I know those men. I'm afraid of them. They've tried to snatch me before… for the white slave trade." Her legs began to tremble.

"My Heavens! I don't dare leave you alone," Mr. Plato exclaimed. "I'll take you home and then you can tell me the whole story. I'd better tell the chief of police."

"The chief of police?" Flora asked. "A Turk?"

"Yes. But don't worry. He's a very good man." Plato reached for his passport, removed the folded letter and handed it to Flora.

The enlarged red seal of Aleppo's Chief of Police stood out at the top of the letter. Flora read the one hand written sentence. *Plato Sawaides is under my personal protection.*

His signature was bold and impressive: *Fikri Bey.*

"He does not want white slavers in his city." Plato took Flora's hands in his. "Now, let's go home."

A week later Mr. Plato told Flora that Fikri Bey had arrested Yanko and the Memoush Oghlou brothers. They were in jail along with four others from Aleppo's white slave gang of seven.

Flora felt safe again, but anguish still tormented her daily. Mr. Plato's happy home was a constant reminder of how wonderful her life had once been. And her fear of being orphaned was a nightmare about to explode. She was desperate to know if her parents were alive. But whenever she asked if there was news of her family, Mr. Plato's response was always the same. "Not yet." Then he'd tell her how much Ambassador Morgenthau was helping the Armenians and how the ambassador had said if Turkey didn't want the Armenians, America would take them. "The ambassador has already made arrangements with a New York philanthropist to donate the first of the 5 million dollars to cover transportation costs," Mr. Plato said, nodded and smiled. "I've been told that the wealthy philanthropist was Morgenthau himself."

That didn't surprise Flora. Miss Webb had told her Ambassador Morgenthau was one of the most humane of men she'd had ever known, and Miss Webb knew a lot of good God fearing Christian men.

But what Flora wanted most from the American Ambassador was information about her family. *Where are they? Are they still alive?*

CHAPTER THIRTY-TWO

ALEPPO SURRENDERS

October 26, 1918.

Three long years had passed, and Flora knew how fortunate she had been to spend those difficult years in the home of the Sawaides family. She had plenty to eat, and her meals were every bit as good as those back home in Hadjin. Most Armenians weren't so lucky. But the war was winding down, and maybe soon she'd know how her own family had fared. She sat crocheting while the two Sawaides children played quietly on the floor. Glancing out the window, she saw Mr. Plato rush up onto the porch. "Papa's home."

The door flew open. A huge smile crossed Mr. Plato's face as he entered. "The British rode into the city under a white flag and demanded Aleppo's surrender."

The needle slipped out of Flora's hand. "You mean the war is over?"

"Not yet. The commander of the Turkish garrison refused. So, there could be fighting. We'd better not leave the house for a few days." He quickly kissed both daughters and rushed away. "I have to tell my wife."

Flora felt her breath quicken. Damascus and Palestine had already been captured, and General Allenby was moving the British army throughout the rest of Syria, pushing Turkish and German forces back into Turkey. Yes! The war would soon be over! But her excitement quickly turned into apprehension. How would she be affected by this turn of world events? For three years she had buried her dreams and let die every seed of hope within her. Now seventeen, she was no longer that high-spirited fourteen year old girl who dared hold the world by its tail. What of her future now? Surprised by the taste of blood, she realized she had been chewing the inside of her lower lip. She pressed her tongue against the cut.

Where would she be a month from now? The war had put her and millions of other innocent people through hell. Being separated from her family was bad enough, but those lost years of study had ruined her chance to attend the American college. When could she go home? Her father had said he'd find her in Aleppo, but where was he and the rest of her family? Then the unthinkable surfaced from the deep recesses of her mind. Her eyes welled. Mr. Plato had deftly avoided answering her questions. She knew the Greek diplomat had asked Aleppo's American consul-general to find the whereabouts of her family through Ambassador Morgenthau, and if the ambassador had found them, Mr. Plato would have told her. She gave up hope when Ambassador Morgenthau returned to America two years ago to help President Wilson win the American President's election. But the main reason the ambassador left Turkey, Mr. Plato had told her, was that Morgenthau was on the verge of a breakdown, so difficult had his job become. He had tried to save the lives of so many, including French, British, and wounded Turkish soldiers, and he had failed in his attempt to persuade the Turkish leaders to release the exiled Armenians to go to America.

Flora understood the depth of that loss. Opportunities in America were unlimited. Her own dreams before the war had taken her to heights she had not thought possible. She had Miss Webb to thank for that. Where was her wonderful teacher? Had she returned to America with Ambassador Morgenthau? And did the ambassador take information about her family with him? Maybe Mr. Plato didn't have the heart to tell her the news she most feared—that her entire family had perished in the desert at Der-el-Zor. Her vision glazed as more tears welled. She picked up her crochet needle from the floor and decided she could do nothing but wait....

An odd silence fell over the city. The Turks may not have surrendered, but the entire garrison fled from Aleppo before the British arrived. Relieved not to witness the bloody fight that would have left soldiers dying on the streets, Flora instead was eager to witness the ceremony where the Syrians presented the city to the British.

On that glorious day Flora felt so proud and happy. Having left the children at home with Mrs. Sawaides, who didn't like being in crowds, Flora and Mr. Plato stood among the multitudes of rejoicing people cramming the area adjacent to the Baron Hotel, where the British had made their headquarters. She wore the handsome new dress Mrs. Sawaides had given her. With her black and white checkered skirt flowing gracefully over her new petticoat and sporting a new white brimmed hat, she felt very European.

The streets were lined with British yeoman in bright red jackets standing at attention as skilled riders of the Australian Light Horse Cavalry, the Indian Cavalry and the Imperial Service Cavalry rode their splendid horses to their assigned places to greet the arrival of General Allenby.

"Look at the fine condition of those horses," Mr. Plato commented to Flora. "They have carried these troops 200 miles in less than two weeks and are far superior to the horses of the Turkish Cavalry."

Flora nodded. But she was far more interested in the Indian Sikh Cavalry. They fascinated her. Big and strong, with long beards and huge turbans covering their hair, she had been told the Sikhs were considered the best of the Indian troops. They no doubt had helped the British become the finest military force in the world.

Her eyes drifted toward the line of British yeomen who stood with the quiet strength that discipline and polish created. Now she understood why England owned a quarter of the world. The British officers certainly were handsome in their clean, neat uniforms. Then her eyes met the striking blue eyes of one of them.

He couldn't take his eyes off her.

Flora grew uncomfortable, but only for a moment. She sensed his look was one of admiration and not a threatening sexual one. Her lips broke into a feminine smile, and she quickly dropped her gaze to her feet. Embarrassed, but flattered, she realized for the first time that she had developed into an attractive young lady. Mr. Plato had told her that several times, but since he was like a father to her, she naturally thought he meant as a father sees his daughter. Now she knew what he meant. She momentarily placed her hand just above her breasts. They had grown and were firm. This was a new Flora, and she wasn't sure how to handle herself, especially in the world where men pursued women. She felt the need to talk to her sister, who had become a stunning nineteen-year-old.

Verkin had refused to attend today's ceremony. She was too scared. Apparently when British soldiers had entered the city and were canvassing the streets looking for enemy, Verkin had inadvertently stepped out on the Shar's balcony. A nervous soldier pointed his rifle at her and she panicked. Crossing herself several times she yelled, "I'm Armenian," shook her head and yelled, "no German!" With her light complexion and auburn hair Verkin did have German features. The soldier lowered his rifle, she ran inside the house and dropped to the floor. Trembling, she stayed down for more than an hour.

Flora understood. Fear had become their constant companion.

"There he is!" Mr. Plato exclaimed. "Now I understand why his troops call him 'The Bull.'"

Flora studied the famed General as he led his cavalry down Baron Street. He was a plain man, but heavily built with a warlike appearance. When Allenby reached the hotel, he dismounted. A Syrian official carrying a silver tray approached him.

Mr. Plato leaned down to Flora. "He is being presented the traditional gold key, bread and salt."

Allenby took the key, held it above his head, and carefully put it back on the tray. Taking the bread, he dipped it into the salt and ate it.

The crowd cheered. Even Flora cheered. The General had accepted their symbol of friendship and hospitality.

"British prestige has never stood higher in the Near East," Mr. Plato said. "And overnight their paper money is being traded at 85% of its face value while the Turkish pound has plummeted to a mere 15%." He laughed. "Fortunately, I've always favored gold."

Now Flora understood why her father had always insisted on receiving payment in gold coins.

* * *

Two weeks later, on November 11, the news spread throughout the city. The armistice had been signed. The Allies had won the war. Now, Flora hoped, life would become normal once again. She loved

Mr. Plato and his family, but she was anxious to go home—to find her parents, her brothers, to have her own happy family, to smell the clean mountain air, to drink Hadjin's sweet spring water, and to walk through the American mission. When would that be? And would Miss Webb be there?

Every morning, as she and Mr. Plato did the day's grocery shopping, Flora searched the streets looking for a familiar face. Armenians by the thousands drifted back to Aleppo, all looking like neglected scrounged animals that had somehow managed to survive in spite of not having shelter or food. She asked every Armenian she saw… do you know Hagop and Arpi Munushian? No one did. They, too, were searching for lost family.

Flora's anxiety grew by the day. She felt as if a heavy, dark cloud pressed upon her, smothering every ounce of hope she had. Would another Christmas pass without being with her family?

Then, three weeks after Christmas, Flora heard a knock at the door of the room she still shared with the cook. Opening it, she stood stunned.

"Hello, Flora," her uncle Mihran said.

Why was her uncle standing there and not her father?

CHAPTER THIRTY-THREE

THE ROAD BACK TO TURKEY

The closed carriage carrying the three passengers stopped in front of Aleppo's railroad station. On this brisk January afternoon, Flora and Verkin were going back to Turkey—to Adana—to live with Uncle Mihran until their mother and father returned. That is, if and when they returned.

Stepping out of the carriage, they each held onto their canvass traveling bags. The only valuable item in Flora's bag was Miss Webb's Bible.

"Stay close," Mihran said, as they passed men hurrying to flag down carriages. He walked to the station's heavy double doors and pushed them open. The girls followed him inside and instantly were surrounded by people rushing to and fro. The station was rank with cigarette smoke.

"We'll wait in the restaurant," Mihran said.

Flora couldn't take her eyes off a well dressed bearded middle-aged man in a long flowing black cape following a porter carrying four pieces of luggage. Directly behind him was an obviously poor Arab boy dragging a heavy bundle tied with rope. She followed Mihran into the already crowded restaurant. Tables were tightly packed together. Some were dirty. Mihran found a clean one and when she and Verkin sat down, he ordered coffee for himself and left to go to the toilet. Flora thought it odd he didn't ask her or Verkin if they wanted anything.

Next to them sat a young European couple. The man's top hat rested on the table, and the attractive blond-haired lady looked uncomfortable in the warm, musty room. Healthy and vibrant, they were in direct contrast to the four sitting at a table opposite them. Flora suspected those four, an older man and woman with two teenage girls, were survivors from the desert. Even in new clothes, they still wore a bedraggled look. The well of gloom within them not only darkened their faces, but also told of their misery. She wondered what atrocities they had survived. She had heard stories, horrible stories, of how forty or more people lived huddled together in the desert caves, and how some were burned alive by the Turks, and how those who had escaped the raging fires were so starved they ate the charred flesh of those who had succumbed. She shuddered. How lucky she had been! Yes, her father had been wise to leave her and her sister in Aleppo, painful as it was to be separated from the family. He said he'd find them in Aleppo, but her uncle had told her he didn't know the whereabouts of her family. But Flora wasn't sure he was telling her the truth.

When Mihran returned, his coffee sat on the table waiting for him. He took a sip and added another spoon of sugar into the demitasse.

A voice over the loudspeaker announced the arrival of a train. People headed for the train's platform.

Flora nudged her uncle. "Is that our train?"

He shook his head. "Not ours." He reached into his vest pocket for his watch.

Flora glanced at four women in black *chadors* leaving the restaurant. "I've never understood why they don't complain, especially during the hot summers. Those *chadors* have to be stifling," Flora said to Verkin.

Verkin nodded, halfheartedly.

"Don't they ever hunger for feminine beauty?" Flora glanced at Verkin. Her sister was elsewhere—in deep thought. Then a picture of the British soldier with the striking blue eyes flashed in Flora's mind. She adjusted her white hat and wondered if she was ready to think of herself as a young feminine lady. She was seventeen. If times had been normal she might have been married and had a baby or two, but then again probably not, because her sights had been set on going to college in America. Now that college was improbable, what options were open to her?

As the four women walked behind a handsome Arab who most likely was their husband, Flora smelled burning tobacco from the lighted cigar in his hand. The four women appeared to be happy.

Flora found herself envying them. Would she ever feel that kind of happiness? Did she dare think of marriage? And hope to find a man as good and kind as Mr. Plato? She again thought of the British soldier. But he wasn't Armenian, and neither was Mr. Plato. Could she marry someone who was not Armenian? She knew she could never marry a Turk. Her hurt and fear of them had festered into a hatred for the whole race. She remembered Miss Webb saying that hatred in your heart prevented you from seeing clearly. But she wanted to hate the Turks... maybe even needed to. Her mind muddled and confused, she didn't want to think anymore.

Unaware she had been chewing her fingernail, she placed her hands on her lap and brushed the skirt of her black and white checkered dress, the one she had worn at the ceremony for General Allenby. In her mind's eye she saw Mr. Plato's smiling face when he told her how lovely she had looked that day. Then she heard a shrill whistle and an announcement of a train's arrival.

Mihran pulled out his watch again. "Right on time. Quickly." He gulped the rest of his coffee and hurried the girls to the wooden platform by the tracks.

Black smoke swirled toward the sky as the train approached. The flag flying from its engine was now British, having replaced the Turkish Crescent moon. When the train came to a full stop, two French soldiers in blue uniforms bounced down the steps and crossed in front of Flora. An admiring glance from one of them unsettled her. His eyes were luminous gray. She deftly stepped behind her uncle.

Suddenly the platform was filled with French soldiers hurrying off the train. Duffel bags braced on their shoulders, they walked briskly away, that is, all except four. They spotted Verkin and stood together, cradling their heavy bags against their necks.

"*Ooo-la-la,*" one said under his breath. Another whistled. "*Ma cherie,*" the tall one commented. The fourth, the only one without a mustache, just stood and gazed at Verkin, his face glowing.

Yes, Flora thought, her sister was the beautiful one. She put her arm around Verkin. "Which one do you want?"

Verkin laughed. "Silly!"

Looking amused, Mihran rushed the girls to board. As Flora stepped up onto the train's vestibule, she turned to see the four soldiers still watching Verkin. They looked like little boys wanting desperately to play.

"Hurry," Mihran said. "Let's find a good seat."

They walked through two cars passing many French soldiers still seated on the train. Flora felt their eyes examining and admiring both her and her sister. In no mood to be bothered by them, Flora looked for seats far away from them. Why were there so many French soldiers? To help the British or to replace them? Before the war the French had brought their culture to both Syria and Lebanon, and Mr. Plato had told Flora that France wanted to act as their protectorate until they achieved independence. How soon would that be? She wondered if Armenia, too, would gain its independence. If so, it would be without Zohrab and Vartkes. She had learned that the two great men had been murdered. That didn't surprise her. Far worse things had been done to thousands of innocent Armenians. She thought of her scholarly brother, Levon. Had he been murdered, too? Her eyes became teary.

She was returning home, but couldn't feel a moment, no not even a breath, of happiness. What was she returning to? Maybe she and Verkin should have stayed in Aleppo and waited for their father. How long would they be expected to stay with her uncle and his family? Flora felt apprehensive about leaving with Mihran, one of her father's five brothers. Except for that time when she visited Uncle Mihran on her way to Constantinople, she barely knew him. The sewing machine he bought with the money Flora's father had sent him saved her uncle from being deported. Instead, the Turks let Mihran stay in Adana and sew army uniforms fourteen to sixteen hours a day. But the deep creases that lined his face said that he hadn't had an easy time, either.

Resting her forehead against the window, Flora watched others climb aboard. A group of young Armenian children were herded onto the train by two ladies who most likely were missionaries. But were they European or American? She knew Near East Relief organizations paid money to those who knew the location of Armenian children who had been bought by Arabs or Kurds. Many of the children did not want to leave their new families, for some lived in loving homes. All had forgotten their native Armenian language and most didn't even know their Armenian names. They were just babies when they were exiled. But the Allied authorities said all Armenians had to return and relearn their culture before it was completely lost. The world needed to know that the attempt to exterminate the Armenian race had failed. But Flora wondered what these children had to look forward to. Living in an orphanage? Their parents, if they survived, would never find them.

And what of her sweet orphans? Were they back in Hadjin? Should she devote her life to them? Her fingernail found its way back into her mouth. Closing her eyes, she hoped to sleep away her unhappiness. A shadow of sadness hung over her.

Sixteen hours later the train arrived in Adana. When the horse carriage stopped in front of Uncle Mihran's home, Flora immediately realized living in this home was not going to be easy. With Mihran's two sons and wife they would be crowded, very crowded in her uncle's home.

Then the Andonian home with all its drudgery flashed in her mind. Why?

CHAPTER THIRTY-FOUR

DEVASTATING NEWS

The next day Flora and Verkin arrived at a home where another surviving uncle stayed with a caretaker. "He was badly hurt in Der-el-Zor," Mihran said as they stood in the courtyard waiting for the door to open. "He's still recovering."

Flora had guessed right. Mihran knew more than he had told her. "He knows about our parents, doesn't he?"

Mihran nodded.

Desperately wanting her family back, Flora found herself chewing her nail again. She yearned to belong to a family. For three years she felt as if she had been an orphan. But as she looked up to see dark clouds forming, she felt as if they were about to swirl down and sweep her away. Then she met her uncle's sad eyes.

"When you see him, try not to be overwhelmed. A blow to his head disfigured his face." He added, "Sometimes he's not coherent."

As Mihran stood in front of one of the entrances where four families shared the simple courtyard, Flora felt her heart racing.

The door opened. A woman said *"parev* (hello)," and Flora and Verkin followed Mihran inside.

"Oh," Flora gasped. Her mouth fell open.

Once tall and robust, her mother's younger brother, Aram, sat slumped in a plain, wooden chair. His bones protruded to such an extent that the outline of his ribs pushed against his shirt. His head hung low and his arms were limp.

Mihran cautiously touched his shoulder.

Aram raised his head. A jagged gash on his head and face had distorted his right eye. It remained half-closed. "Is that Flora? And Verkin?" he asked, a smile trying to cross his bony face.

Flora broke into tears. So did Verkin.

Then Uncle Aram began to sob. "I can't stop crying. My loved ones follow and call after me. They want to hug and take me with them. They look for me in the river. I can't sleep." He wiped his eyes with his hands and tried to slow down his heaving sobs. Wheezes rang through his long breaths. "The soldiers opened fire. They were like wild beasts!" His hands flew up and squeezed his ears tight. "I still hear the screaming... and quick whips from the swords. Women, children," he sobbed, "everyone crying for help." He sobbed again and again. "God didn't hear. He was deaf."

"Come, Aram," the woman said, grasping his arm. "Time to rest."

"I don't want to live," Aram said. "I don't want to live," he repeated as the woman helped him onto a cot in the corner of the room.

"We should go," Mihran said.

Flora reached for her sister. Verkin was crying. Both girls, discombobulated, followed their uncle outside.

Now sobbing, Flora rested the side of her face on Verkin's shoulder. Her tears had dampened her sister's blouse. She turned toward Mihran and demanded, "Mother and Father are dead, aren't they?"

Mihran nodded.

"When... where?" Flora grasped Verkin's hand.

"Are you sure you want to know?"

Heartbroken, grieving and overcome, neither girl could answer.

"Let's go home first," Mihran said.

Later that day Mihran told the girls about Uncle Aram's tragedy, and its fateful interlocking with their parents and brothers. "Aram couldn't talk about it at first," Mihran said, "but finally he told me." He took a deep breath and appeared as if he didn't want to tell the girls the whole story.

"I want to know," Flora demanded.

"Me, too," Verkin echoed.

"All right. All right." Mihran wiped his brow with the back of his hand. "Your parents had camped with thousands of others by the Euphrates. As the sun rose that terrible morning last September, armed soldiers marched into the camp. Everyone panicked. They ran in every direction." He turned his head away. "The soldiers killed thirteen thousand Armenians that morning."

"Our family?" Flora asked.

"Every one of them." Mihran answered and paused. "Siran's family, too."

Flora tried to hold back her tears. Not Verkin, however. Hers flowed uncontrollably.

"Aram and twenty others jumped into the river," Mihran continued. "But as they crossed to the other side...." He shook his head.

Flora grasped his arm. "Tell us!"

Mihran looked at one pair of anguished eyes and then the other. He took a deep breath. "When they got to the other side and started up the bank, now Arabs came after them swinging sickles and swords."

"My God!" Verkin gasped.

"Arabs?" Flora asked, looking confused.

"I don't understand, either," Mihran said. "The Turks must have paid them."

Stunned and choked, neither Flora nor Verkin could say anything.

"Thinking Aram dead," Mihran continued, "they tied rocks to his feet and threw him into the river with thousands of dead bodies. The river was red with blood." Mihran stopped for a moment. "But Aram managed to free himself. He floated downstream. He said the air was heavy with death. Finally, after eight hours he pulled himself out of the water and hid for two days. Then he fell unconscious. When he awoke two Bedouins were wrapping his wounds. They were infested with maggots."

"But the war was almost over," Flora screamed. "Why kill those helpless people?"

"Why? Probably because they hate us," Mihran said.

"Hate a little boy like Avedis? And Dickran, Toros, Mother-Father!" Flora crumpled to the floor.

Verkin put her own unsteady arms around Flora. Trying to lift her, she, too, fell. They grasped each other, wanting to ease the pain.

"Levon. Does anyone know if he's alive?" Verkin managed to ask.

Mihran shook his head. "My guess is he was sent to a labor battalion. Not one of those boys has returned."

Flora knew that to be true. In Aleppo she never saw any young men among the stream of refugees. And she so loved Levon, her book-loving brother. Oh, Levon! Her heart felt as if it would break. And then, like a bolt of lightening, her deepest fear surfaced.

She was an orphan.

CHAPTER THIRTY-FIVE

A DESPAIRING MARRIAGE

The knowledge that her family would never return shattered Flora, but the loss of her father was the toughest for her to bear. Never again would she hold his hand or feel his protective strength or smell tannin when he walked into the house after curing his newly purchased hides. Downcast and dispirited, her mind still felt heavy, even after six months of having heard the heart sickening news.

Another burden clouded her life.

Uncle Mihran turned out not to be such a nice man. He was oppressive and yelled constantly, especially at his wife. He had none of the kindness of her father. Flora couldn't understand how the two men could have been brothers. Mihran had a mean streak as bad as Mrs. Andonian's. His complaining voice barked at her at least once every other day. Do you know how much money it costs me to keep you here?

Flora decided she had to confront him. Her brother, Antranig, had been sending money from America, but her uncle never told her or Verkin. She found out from someone who had seen him pick up the money from the postal center.

She yearned to be free from her uncle. But how? Maybe she should write to Antranig and ask him to send the money directly to her or Verkin. Then she and her sister could go to Hadjin, and she could go back to school. But was the family home still vacant? The Turkish government had declared Armenian homes abandoned and had given them to Turkish families. Some Armenians had already returned to Hadjin and had reclaimed their homes, but it was not an easy process. The French, who were given the *honor* of occupying Cilician Armenia, determined by arbitration the owners of the homes.

But it was safer for Flora to stay in Adana, where a French battalion protected the city. Turkish soldiers had regrouped under their new leader, Mustafa Kemal. They hadn't yet attacked Hadjin, but everyone feared they would.

What could she do? Where was her life going? Her whole purpose during the war was to rejoin her family, and before that awful time she had hoped her education would give her the independence she so craved. Those hopes had slipped away. She had to force herself to look ahead. But, to what?

Hearing the door slam, she knew Mihran had come home. In her mind she mimicked his insensitive platitude, *Do you know how much money you're costing me?* and chuckled.

"Flora?" he called.

Surprised how pleasant his voice sounded, she answered,

"Yes, uncle," and walked into the front room. He held a letter in his hand.

"From Antranig?"

He shook his head and extended the letter.

Flora seized it, tore it open and quickly read it. Her face exploded into a huge smile. "It's from Miss Webb! She says there's a scholarship for me to resume my studies and that I can live at the orphanage... for free! The heaviness that had lived with her for all these months dissolved in that moment. "Miss Webb wants me to come to Hadjin!" She threw her hands high in the air.

"Let me see." Mihran reached for the letter as Flora lowered her arms. Scanning it, he said, "The time may not be right." His voice was harsh.

Flora shot him a cold look. "Why? Are you afraid if I leave, my brother won't send you any more money!" She snatched the letter, stormed out of the house and slammed the door, just like her uncle always did.

Today was Flora's day to care for the children, but she didn't think twice about leaving them alone with their mean, old father. Her angry heart pounded and she heard every beat. She needed to talk to her sister.

Verkin was visiting Krikor and Siran who had also found their way to Adana. Siran was desperately trying to regain a respectable image now that the war was over. Everyone knew she had escaped Der-el-Zor by working in a brothel.

Verkin will be happy for me, she thought. Siran, too. And especially Krikor. Flora loved Krikor dearly. She never forgot his bravery on that dreadful day when she had been taken to the harem.

Hurrying through the winding dirt streets, Flora was breathing more easily when she arrived at Siran's small apartment. Siran was biding her time until her husband sent enough money to buy passage to America for her and Krikor. She looked up to see Krikor's smiling face pressed against the window.

Krikor opened the door. "Hi, Flora."

She returned his smile and rushed into the room waving the letter. She thrust it into her sister's hands. "It's from Miss Webb. She's in Hadjin!"

Verkin quickly read the letter. Her face paled. "Are you going?"

"Yes!"

Verkin handed the letter to Siran. "Maybe, you should think about it first."

Flora wrinkled her brow. "You're not happy for me?"

"You'll be leaving me," Verkin said.

Flora's mouth dropped open. Staring at her sister, she recalled the difficult days on the march, the attempted rape, the loneliness she felt in Adana when chickens were her only companions, and the courage Verkin had shown the night she rescued Flora from the harem. Flora hadn't considered how Verkin would feel, so excited was she about going back to school.

"There's something else you should think about," Siran said and handed the letter back to Flora. "Hadjin is vulnerable. The French have left to fight the Turks who are constantly attacking the city of Marash."

Flora barely heard her. She was still thinking about the overwhelming loneliness she felt these last three years and hadn't considered that Verkin would be lonely without her. She didn't know what to do.

Later, when Flora and Verkin returned to their uncle's home, Mihran refused to speak to either of them that night and for another two days.

"He's giving us the silent treatment," Flora said.

Verkin smiled. "It's wonderful not to hear his complaining voice."

But little did Verkin know how that silent treatment would affect her life.

When Mihran arrived home from work on that third day, he opened the door and called out, "Verkin! I have news for you."

Not liking the sound of his voice, Flora followed her sister into the front room.

"Ahh, both of you are here. Good. You need to hear what I have to say." A gloating smile on his face, he approached Verkin and lifted her chin. "You are a lucky girl. Next month you will marry Hrant Manoogian."

"What!" Verkin screamed and twisted her head away.

Flora grabbed her uncle's arm. "She's engaged to Armen."

"Ohh," Mihran said. "Has he returned?" He turned his head in every direction as if looking for the young man. "I don't see him." He raised his hand and slapped Flora across her face.

Stunned, Flora lunged backward. Her cheek stung.

Mihran slapped his hand against Verkin's shoulder. "Hrant has asked for you, I said yes, and that's that!"

"No! I won't marry him!"

"Oh, yes, you will," Mihran said, pushing Verkin against the wall.

His wife ran into the room. "Mihran...."

"Leave us alone," he screamed, thrusting his hand toward her.

His wife slowly backed away.

"I won't marry him!" Verkin screamed. "He's too old!" Tears streamed down her face. "I won't. I won't!"

Mihran stormed out of the room. Returning, he held tightly the leather strap he used to sharpen his razor. Suddenly he raised it and snapped it against Verkin's back. His face was beet red.

"Stop!" Flora yelled as Mihran raised the strap again.

Mihran turned, whacked Flora once, dropped the strap and marched out of the house. He slammed the door.

Shaken, the two girls stood crying.

"What can we do?" Flora put her arm around Verkin. "It's not fair."

Mihran's wife, holding the hands of her two youngest, came back into the room. She, too, was weeping. "It's not right we women have so little control over our lives." Trying to console Verkin, she said, "Try to look ahead. Your children will bring you joy."

Flora watched her helpless sister kiss her aunt and crumple to the floor. What other choice did Verkin have? To live on the streets?

* * *

In August, one month later, Verkin stood in front of the altar of the Gregorian church in Adana. Flora was her maid of honor. There were no bridesmaids. The ceremony took an hour. Darkness shadowed Verkin's beautiful face. Wearing a simple white dress, Verkin had refused the expensive lace gown Hrant's parents wanted to have made for the wedding. Flora knew why. It was the only way her nineteen-year old sister could show her defiance. Verkin loved beautiful clothes and would have chosen an elegant gown had she been marrying Armen back home in Hadjin and in ordinary circumstances.

Her sister deserved better. Hrant was twice Verkin's age and was already losing his hair. It wasn't that Hrant was a bad man, he just didn't have a lot of polish. Flora thought Hrant was somewhat slow and wondered if his parents, who owned a fine fabric shop, had paid Mihran a nice sum to have Verkin marry their son. Then a fearful thought crossed her mind. Would her uncle do the same to her? She'd be eighteen soon.

Later, after the reception dinner at Hrant's parent's home, Flora sat watching her uncle as he drank coffee. Had he made similar marriage plans for her? Determined not to be sold to the highest bidder, she decided to confront him. Mentally she chewed over what she'd say to him… *You have no right to choose who I'll marry… I'll leave and go back to Hadjin… I'll write to Antranig and ask him to send me a boat ticket to America. Maybe she could go with Siran and Krikor. They'd be leaving soon.* Flora grew more anxious with every thought.

When it was time to leave, she hugged Verkin goodbye. She didn't have the heart to congratulate her sister and wish her the best. Verkin was too distressed. Flora felt Verkin's tears drip against her cheeks. She kissed Verkin's damp eyes, turned and left the house. She waited outside for her uncle and his wife.

"Uncle," she called as he approached. "I hope you're not trying to find me a husband too!" Her voice was challenging.

"You!" he said through a laugh. "Nobody wants you!" He walked away, still laughing.

Stunned, grateful, and sad, all at the same time, Flora wondered what was behind the cutting remark.

Why would he say that?

CHAPTER THIRTY-SIX

A CONFRONTATION

Flora didn't sleep well that night. Her mind was consumed with her uncle's comment. What did he mean? Why wouldn't a nice Armenian boy want her for a wife? Not that she wanted to get married, that is, not yet, anyway, and certainly not to anyone her uncle would choose for her, but she didn't like the feeling of being a castoff. That's how orphans felt.

What of her orphaned mission friends, Ana and Sona? Did they feel that way too? But she knew their situation was serious and maybe even dangerous. At least she hadn't been snared into a life of harlotry. Hmmm. Harlotry... did Uncle Mihran think she worked in the brothel with her cousin, Siran?

No! Impossible. How could anyone think that of her? She was Flora, who loved education. It had to be something else. Maybe... the harem and Ahmed Pasha? She'd confront Uncle Mihran tomorrow. Yes. Tomorrow. She pulled the blanket over her head, wanting to hide from the world.

All the next day Flora waited anxiously for Mihran to return home. She heard the door slam, hurried to the front room and waited for her uncle to remove his hat.

"What do you want, Flora?"

"I've been thinking about what you said last night."

"Ohhh."

"I don't know what you mean."

"You don't?" Mihran's face broke into a sardonic grin.

Flora backed away.

"Why are you acting so surprised?" he asked. "But then I suppose your kind likes to keep those things secret."

"Secret?" Bewildered, Flora wanted to shake her uncle until he explained himself. She reached toward him and immediately pulled her hand back, remembering the beating he had given Verkin. She froze. His hand was coming toward her.

Mihran lifted her chin, squeezed it and peered deeply into Flora's unsteady eyes. "Armenian men want virgins for wives."

Her head reeling, Flora felt faint.

"By the way, now that Verkin is gone, you'll have to do her work, also. You know, it costs me a lot of money to keep you here."

Dazed, Flora watched him leave. "You're an ugly, old man," she murmured to herself. "And I'm going to get away from you."

* * *

The following afternoon when Flora finished her chores, she sneaked out of her uncle's home. She needed to confide in her sister.

Wearing a plain blue cotton dress, Flora rushed through the Adana streets. Verkin's new home, where she lived with Hrant and his family, was a good distance away. She wiped perspiration off her brow, a reminder she didn't like the hot, humid Adana summers. Even the nights didn't turn cool.

She glanced at the clock tower in the middle of the outdoor bazaar. Seven minutes past five. Mihran would be home soon and wonder where she had gone. She didn't care. She was determined not to let her uncle rule her life.

Passing shoemakers fixing shoes, tin makers pounding and shaping metal, and hawkers selling goods far inferior to those in Aleppo's famous bazaar, she approached the old Roman bridge crossing the Seyhan River. She smelled seared lamb. Turning, she noticed a man across the street in front of a small restaurant. He was grilling long skewers of kebabs over hot cinders. She inhaled the wonderful aroma, remembering the awful pangs of hunger on the march.

Twenty minutes later she stood in front of Hrant's parents' home. She hesitated. Should she knock? After all, Verkin had been married for only two days. Turning to leave, she stopped, thought of Uncle Mihran and decided she had to talk to her sister.

Just then the door opened. "Flora, is something wrong?" Verkin asked.

Tears welled in her eyes.

"Come inside."

Flora looked longingly at Verkin, hugged her sister and entered the neat home. She sat in the overstuffed chair closest to the door and heard Hrant's mother's voice.

"Whose there, Verkin?"

"My sister," she answered and stroked Flora's long brown hair.

"How nice," the woman said as she entered the room. "Oh, my dear, Flora. You look like a little bird who has been bruised. What's wrong?"

"I need to talk to Verkin," Flora responded, holding back the tears that wanted to spill down her cheeks.

Mrs. Manoogian smiled. "Of course." Before turning to leave, she said, "Join us for dinner, if you like."

"Thank you."

Mrs. Manoogian's halting gait suggested she felt uneasy leaving the two girls.

"She's a kind lady," Verkin said as she bent down to meet Flora's troubled eyes. "Now, tell me!"

Flora tried to smile. "How is everything with you?"

"All right, I guess."

Flora kissed Verkin's eyes. This day should have been a fun loving time—talking about the wedding night and how excited they'd be about Verkin's future. But these were strange times and would never fill the happiness the war had destroyed.

"They treat me well," Verkin said, "but I can't stop thinking about... how it could have been."

"Me, too." Now the tears streamed down Flora's cheeks. "Uncle Mihran's telling everyone I'm not a virgin!"

"What!" Verkin gently braced her hands against Flora's wet face. "How could he?"

"I don't want to live with him any longer."

"Damn him!" Verkin paced the room. Suddenly she stopped. "Write to Miss Webb. Go to Hadjin."

Flora hugged and kissed her sister. "I wouldn't go without your blessing."

"I'll miss you, but... I want what's best for you."

Flora kissed Verkin again. "I don't want to leave you. But with all the chores Uncle is forcing on me now that you're gone, I'd probably never have time to see you. And you have a new family."

Verkin took Flora's hand and pulled her to the small desk in the corner of the room. "Write the letter!"

That night when Flora returned, Uncle Mihran was furious. "Who do you think you are, Miss high and mighty? Don't ever leave this house without my permission again!" He stood over Flora, his hand high above her face.

Flora backed away.

"UNDERSTAND?!"

"Yes, Uncle." Her eyes filled with apprehension, Flora knew she had to be submissive. His hand was still in striking position.

Mihran lowered his hand, reached into his shirt pocket for a cigarette and stormed out of the house.

Flora's knees grew weak.

"Are you all right?" Mihran's wife asked from the kitchen.

"Yes." Flora could hardly get the word out of her mouth.

"Sometimes... if he doesn't know everything... he loses his good sense," Mihran's wife said. She came into the room and embraced Flora. "He'll be better tomorrow."

Flora hoped he'd give her the silent treatment.

And he did—for four days.

A month went by. Flora turned eighteen. Still no response from Miss Webb. And news filtering out of Hadjin was bad. The Turks had attacked. The battle continued with no end in sight. Then the news came.

Miss Webb had been shot and died from her wounds.

"Why her?" she shouted to Verkin. "She's not Armenian!"

Stroking Flora's hair, Verkin whispered, "I know. I know." She drew Flora's head against her bosom and rocked her like a bruised infant who had been abandoned. "A bullet flying through the air doesn't know if it hit a baby, a girl, a boy, an Armenian, or an American."

Flora dried her damp cheek on her sister's shoulder." I have to get away from that man."

"I know. I know." Verkin drew Flora back to her bosom. "Maybe you can live here, with us. But it's too soon to ask."

Flora was too weak to respond. She stayed for dinner, the mood somber. Her despondency was obvious to Mr. and Mrs. Manoogian. Flora deftly avoided their questions. How could she bring up the subject of her sexual purity?

As Hrant and his father escorted her back to Mihran's home, they walked along the winding streets in silence. She wished her father was walking beside her instead of Mr. Manoogian... to hold his hand and to hear his wise advice... she longed to talk to her father.

When they reached Mihran's house, Mr. Manoogian knocked softly on the front door.

The door opened and Mihran, a lit cigarette hanging from his mouth, appeared surprised to see them.

"Hello, Mihran. I'm returning your charge." Mr. Manoogian pushed Flora gently and followed her inside.

Mihran shot Flora a look that said *you have disobeyed me again*. He closed the door, reached for the package of cigarettes in his pocket and offered one to each of the men. Both took a cigarette and lighted up.

"Coffee?" Mihran asked.

"No, thank you. My wife is expecting us. Her sister's family is coming over." Mr. Manoogian turned to Flora. "Visit us again... soon." He shook Mihran's hand. "Good-bye."

"Bye Flora." Hrant said.

Flora watched the two men walk up the street, closed the door and turned to see that Mihran had left the room. Had he gone for the razor strap?

She rushed to the closet and quickly pulled out her folding mat and blanket and set them on the floor next to Mihran's two youngest who were sound asleep. She lay down, clothes and all, pulled the blanket over her head, and listened for her uncle's footsteps.

They never came.

CHAPTER THIRTY SEVEN

A CHANGE

Early the next morning Flora heard the door slam shut. She glanced at the clock on the wall. Not quite six. Why had Mihran left so early?

"Go back to sleep," she said to Mihran's two young sons. "You don't have to get up for another hour." She tucked the boys' blankets around their shoulders and went into the kitchen.

Mihran's wife sat at the table drinking a cup of tea. "Did you sleep in your dress?"

"Oh, Auntie, I don't know what to do."

"Sit down. Tell me all about it." Mihran's wife handed her a cup of hot tea.

Cradling the warm cup, Flora took a sip and poured out her heart, spilling her hurt like a dam whose walls had cracked open... how could anyone think she was capable of something so shameful and how could she save her honor?

"Oh, my dear... then you really are a virgin."

The remark startled Flora. If Auntie and Uncle Mihran believed it, did the whole community think she was impure? "What can I do?" she pleaded, pressing the back of her aunt's hand.

"I'm not sure."

"But it's a terrible lie!"

Auntie shrugged. "These have been difficult times... so many lies, so many dead, so many hearts broken."

Yes, her heart had been broken again, and regardless of the truth, Flora knew the lie would hang out there and blacken her chances for a good marriage. But if she got away from her uncle, then maybe the smear wouldn't follow her." Auntie... I hope you understand. Verkin is going to ask the Manoogians if I can live with them."

"Oh, dear."

"Uncle Mihran makes my life miserable... uh... why did he leave so early this morning?"

"A job out of town. He'll be back next week."

"Oh, Auntie, I won't leave you alone, it's just that Uncle is so mean to me."

"He's not always so harsh, Flora. There are times when he's extremely gentle. He just doesn't show it often... thinks it's unmanly."

Flora wondered why Mihran felt he had to be intimidating. Her father, Mr. Plato, and Captain Khourshid were kind and compassionate men, yet well respected, especially for their moral strength. If only Uncle Mihran understood th... at, she wouldn't feel the need to escape from him.

"Oh, Auntie," Flora begged, "Please... help me make the lie go away."

* * *

That next week when Mihran was away, Flora discussed with her aunt how they would tell her uncle she was leaving, that is, if and when Verkin's new family said she could live with them.

"I don't want our community looking badly upon Mihran," Auntie said. "After all, he is your uncle and it's his responsibility to care for you... until you are married."

Her uncle's cutting words rang through her mind.... Who wants you? God forbid she'd have to live with him forever. "I've thought about that, too, Auntie, but I think I've an explanation for my leaving that the community will understand."

"Tell me."

"Too many changes too quickly."

"Go on."

"Well, you know how hard both of us took the loss of our family. It still hurts. And now with a new marriage, Verkin needs stability of family... me... at least for a while... until she adjusts to her new life."

"That rings true," Auntie said.

It is true, Flora thought. Her sister needed her as much as she needed Verkin. "If Uncle thinks my move is temporary... more for

Verkin than for me, he won't be offended. And, who knows, maybe the community will even praise him for such action." She wondered if she had stretched too much with that last statement.

* * *

Two months later, at the end of October, Flora moved in with the Manoogians. And, yes, just as Flora had predicted, Mihran told everyone that Verkin had become despondent and needed the company of her sister for a while.

But Verkin was depressed. She hadn't yet adjusted to her new life, even though she was treated kindly. Flora lifted Verkin's spirits whenever she could. Those moments were easiest in the fabric shop, when they were left in charge. Surrounded by lovely silks, linens, cottons and woolen textiles, they draped the various fabrics around each other, creating mostly silly fashions. But once in a while, Verkin's face beamed with happiness when one of her creations turned Flora into a fashionable young woman.

The girls became closer than ever. But even after five months, Flora still felt like a stranger in the Manoogian home. She didn't really belong and longed to feel family roots of her own.

She hated being an orphan.

CHAPTER THIRTY-EIGHT

A MYSTERIOUS VISITOR

On their way home after having worked the morning shift in the fabric shop, Flora and Verkin took a walk through a small park. A gentle rain had cleaned the air. Birds chirped as they flew from branch to branch. Trees and flowers were bursting with joy. Spring had arrived.

Throwing small pieces of bread on the grass under a sycamore tree, the two girls watched black crows swoop down and chase away the smaller birds scrambling for the scraps. *Birds never go hungry,* Flora thought and smiled. Apricot and cherry blossoms had already fallen, and when the fruit matured the birds would find the ripe ones before the humans did. Flora loved the invigorating energy of the season.

Verkin, too, responded to the elixir of Spring. Her depression had eased, and for the first time in years, she looked forward to the future. She was pregnant and happy to be.

"We probably should hurry." Verkin said. "I wonder who this lady is that Hrant's mother wants us to meet."

"I'm curious, too. When they arrived home and opened the door, Flora's eyes fell on the mysterious woman sitting very straight in the comfortable overstuffed chair. Her strong, squared face and jaw were in contrast to her small brown eyes. Her hair was parted in the middle and pulled back into a bun. She wore a black embroidered blouse with a simple, long black skirt.

"Girls, I want you to meet Khatoon Ketlegian," Mrs. Manoogian said. She took their hands and walked them to the regal looking woman.

"Ah, yes, Verkin. You are as beautiful as everyone says." Khatoon Ketlegian patted Verkin's stomach and smiled. "How soon?"

"Five more months... towards the end of August."

"And you must be Flora." The woman stood and looked Flora up and down, much like a buyer sizing up a horse. "You're not as tall as your sister."

"No, I'm not," Flora responded with a tinge of anger. She stretched, trying to reach the five feet she hadn't yet met.

After a few minutes of small talk, Mrs. Manoogian abruptly asked the girls, "Can you make us coffee?"

"Of course," both responded in unison.

Flora felt the request was a ploy to get them out of the room. "What's your mother-in-law up to?"

Verkin laughed. "We'll soon find out."

Ten minutes later and carrying a small tray filled with baklava, Flora followed her sister back into the room. As the four sat sipping their coffee, eating the sweet pastry, and coyly glancing at one another Flora began to feel uneasy.

Finally, Mrs. Manoogian broke the silence. "Mrs. Ketlegian will be leaving for America soon... to join her son."

Flora's ears perked up. "How wonderful."

The cultured woman smiled. Her strong face softening, her eyes alert.

Flora felt the woman was observing her every movement. She grew more uncomfortable and set down her demitasse, still half full of coffee.

"Yes," Mrs. Manoogian said. "And her son wants her to bring him a nice Armenian girl he can marry."

Flora and Verkin simultaneously moved to the edge of their chairs.

"My sister will make a wonderful wife," Verkin said.

Flora felt blood drain from her face. Did she dare hope? *America. America.*

Mrs. Ketlegian opened her purse. "My son, Sarkis." She handed a photograph to Verkin, who was sitting next to her.

"Hmmm. Nice looking. How old is he?" She handed the photo to Flora.

"Just turned twenty-seven."

Flora thought his age was good—old enough to be steady, but not too old. She liked his looks, especially his thick, dark hair. His nose and mouth were just like those of his mother. She looked directly at Mrs. Ketlegian's large nose and then back to the photograph, remembering an outrageous statement her father had once made— that big noses and intelligence were synonymous.

"My son is not very tall," Mrs. Ketlegian said. "The two of you will look good together."

Flora didn't know what to say. The woman liked her because she was short? She hated her littleness... thought it was a detriment... now her small body could take her to America.

"He said whoever I chose will be fine, but... " Mrs. Ketlegian said and paused. "He has one requirement."

"Oh." Flora tried to appear stoic, but her insides were quivering.

"Yes. He said he doesn't want anyone's *leftovers.*" The woman reached over Verkin and touched Flora. "Will you be willing to be examined by a mid-wife."

"Of course, of course," Flora said softly, but she wanted to jump up screaming *"Yes"* and thought, *My God, she hasn't heard the rumors.*

"Will tomorrow be all right?

Flora glanced at Mrs. Manoogian, who nodded her approval.

"Tomorrow will be fine."

"Until then." Mrs. Ketlegian rose and hugged Flora. "You are a pretty little thing. My Sarkis is going to love you."

As the strong, stately woman released her grip, Flora held back the laughter that wanted to explode from her body. She tightened her grip on the photo of the good looking young man from America, fearing her suppressed emotions would spill over and ruin this wonderful opportunity. Her heart was racing.

"Tomorrow afternoon... One o'clock?"

Nodding, Flora tried to hand her the photo.

"No. You keep it." She brushed her hand across Flora's cheek. "I like you."

Flora didn't dare open her mouth. If she burst into laughter the woman might think she was crazy. Instead, she managed to hug Mrs. Ketlegian goodbye.

When Mrs. Manoogian closed the door behind the visitor, Flora fell onto the couch and burst into tears.

"I thought you'd be happy," a stunned Mrs. Manoogian said.

"She is," Verkin said, patting Flora's eyes with a handkerchief. "These are tears of joy!"

CHAPTER THIRTY NINE

AN EXAMINATION

Nervously brushing her hair in front of the mirror in Mrs. Manoogian's bedroom, Flora glanced at the clock on the dresser. One o'clock exactly. Then she heard the knock and Mrs. Manoogian's friendly greeting. She clasped her hands in prayer. "God... don't let anything go wrong, *pleeease.*"

"Flora, Mrs. Ketlegian is here."

She stood as tall as she could, stroked the brush through her hair one more time, straightened her long blue skirt, took a deep breath and marched into the front room as if she had been victorious in battle. Her stomach was in knots.

A plain looking woman, around twenty-five, stood next to Mrs. Ketlegian. Flora assumed she was the mid-wife.

"She's perfect for Sarkis," the young woman said, her face beaming.

"Flora, This is Berjoohy. She's married to my son, Raffi. I don't think I told you I have three sons and a daughter."

She hadn't, but Flora had learned a great deal about the Ketlegian family since yesterday. Khatoon Ketlegian, a widow of many years, was from a family of landowners and had come from Talas, one of the wealthier sections of Turkey, but like so many Armenians, she had lost everything. The day before her family was deported, Mrs. Ketlegian gave the family deeds to a Greek woman for safekeeping, but the woman and her family were nowhere to be found.

Mrs. Ketlegian, her two sons and daughter-in-law, decided to stay in Adana where it was still safe to live. Years before, in 1913, she had sent her son, Sarkis, to accompany her only daughter to Boston where she was to be wed. Now Sarkis was their hope. He could sponsor them all to America.

"Welcome, Berjoohy," Flora said. "Are you the mid-wife?"

Berjoohy smiled. "Yes."

Feeling uncomfortable, Flora wished Verkin was here. She needed her sister's support, but Mrs. Manoogian felt the fewer people, the better.

"Use my room," Mrs. Manoogian said.

Flora forced a smile.

"Shall we?" Berjoohy asked.

Perspiration beaded on Flora's forehead as she and Berjoohy left for the bedroom.

Minutes later the two girls reappeared. Berjoohy gave Mrs. Ketlegian a nod.

Flora, happy and embarrassed, managed to smile. She ran her hands through her long hair and tried to appear confident. But the dampness that had built up on her white cotton blouse, especially under her arms, betrayed that image.

Mrs. Ketlegian rushed to Flora and whisked her in her arms. "I'm so happy."

Flora tried to remain calm.

Releasing her grip, Mrs. Ketlegian said, "Tomorrow we'll go to the French authorities for traveling permits. It will be much easier if I say you are my daughter. Is that all right?"

Nodding, Flora was still too unsettled to speak.

"Tomorrow, then. I'll come for you in the morning." She stroked Flora's cheek. "My sweet little Flora."

The woman had struck a treasured memory. Those were the same words her beloved father always said... my sweet little Flora.

Did she dare hope another well of lovingness would come into her life?

FORTY

IN DEMAND

The two women finally left. Flora's face showed the strain of the afternoon.

"It's not every day a nice Armenian girl like you finds a husband in America," Mrs. Manoogian said with a loving smile. "I'm happy for you, and I know Verkin will be too." She patted Flora's shoulder. "Let's fix something special for dinner. To celebrate!"

Flora was overcome with gratitude. Verkin's kind mother-in-law never doubted her, and she'd forever feel indebted to her. Even though her dreams of an education would never materialize, she at least would enter a door into the New World. She had Mrs. Manoogian to thank for that.

As she cut pieces of lamb for stew and Mrs. Manoogian kneaded dough for cheese *boreg,* she heard the front door swing open.

"Flora!" Verkin cried out. "Are you going to America?"

Flora flew out of the kitchen and rushed into her sister's arms. They stayed locked together. Neither could say the words that were in their hearts… the vast separation… .they might never see each other. But Flora knew she had to go to America.

Releasing her grasp, she was surprised to see Uncle Mihran standing by the open door.

"What's this I hear? You're going to America?"

She watched Mihran walk into the house and close the door.

"Congratulations, my wonderful little niece. I'm happy for you." He approached her and before she could react, he pinched her cheek. "I knew it all the time. That man in Boston is fortunate to have you, especially since so many of our poor girls were raped by those terrible Turkish beasts."

Flora restrained her urge to spit in his face.

"Now, don't forget us, dear Flora. Maybe your new husband can sponsor us too. I'd love to go to America."

Verkin shot him a curt look. "Are you including me?"

"Naturally," Mihran said, red blush becoming visible on his face.

There was a loud knock. Flora opened the door.

"*Parev* (Hello)," said the well-dressed woman facing her. Mrs. Adamian, also from Hadjin, had a son the same age as Flora. Her two older sons never returned from the exile. She stepped inside and greeted Mihran. "You have such lovely nieces."

"Yes, I do." He lifted his chin. "Have you heard? Flora is going to America."

"Really? She's made up her mind already?"

"Yes," Mihran responded and turned toward Flora. "My wonderful little niece."

The woman looked alarmed. "Can we talk privately, my child?" She approached Flora and stroked her shiny hair.

"Yes, of course."

Mihran, a curious look on his face, hesitated. "Should I leave you two together?"

Flora nodded.

"Hmmm. Well, I'll say hello to Verkin's mother-in-law. Is she in the kitchen? I smell something wonderful cooking."

Flora nodded again.

"I'm so excited for you." He strutted toward the kitchen like a peacock showing off his feathers.

Flora wanted to burst into laughter, but didn't dare. Mrs. Adamian would think her rude. Then she thought it odd the woman was here. Why? Certainly not to offer her son in marriage. She'd had more than a year to do that. But... then, had she heard about the examination? And how did Uncle Mihran find out? It had been only three hours since Mrs. Ketlegian and Berjoohy had left.

"I'll join Uncle in the kitchen," Verkin said and winked as she left her sister alone with Mrs. Adamian.

"Is it true, Flora? You've decided to go to America?" Mrs. Adamian asked.

Flora met the woman's eyes, questioning why it concerned her.

"A nice Hadjin girl like you should marry a boy from Hadjin. That's been our tradition. Hadjin girls marry Hadjin boys."

Flora sat on the couch and waited for the woman to settle in the overstuffed chair. She knew what was coming.

"You shouldn't rush into these matters so quickly," Mrs. Adamian said. "Marriage is for life, and America is so far away. You'll never see your sister or uncle again. Maybe you should stay here. There are many fine Hadjin boys, like my son." She hesitated. "Maybe you should consider marrying him. I know my boy. He'll make a fine husband."

"Your son is very nice, I agree. I've always liked him." But in her mind Flora knew why it took this well-respected *dandigin* (lady of the house) more than a year to approach her. More than likely she, like all the others, had questioned her virginity.

"You know, my dear Flora, it's not well known, but we haven't lost everything. I was able to leave my jewelry and some gold in the English bank here in Adana before the exile. You'll be comfortable in our home, especially when we return to Hadjin."

There was another knock.

Flora opened the door to see Mrs. Kalustian, another woman from Hadjin. She had two marriageable sons. Mrs. Kalustian reached out and hugged Flora so tightly Flora could hardly breathe. "*Yavrum.*" ("My sweet").

"Come in," Flora said, closed the door behind them, and watched the woman's face explode in surprise when she saw Mrs. Adamian.

"Ohhh... hello." Mrs. Kalustian nodded to the woman sitting in the overstuffed chair.

Mrs. Adamian managed a weak smile.

"If this is not a good time, Flora, I'll return another day. I have a very private matter I'd like to discuss with you." Mrs. Kalustian stroked Flora's arm and gave the other woman a snippety look.

"No. Please stay. Mrs. Adamian was just leaving. Aren't you?" Flora asked.

Before the first woman could answer, Mihran reentered and greeted the new visitor. "Have you heard? My wonderful little niece is going to America!" He reached out to pinch Flora again.

Flora backed away. "I'm… not… a… child." Her voice was firm.

"Absolutely correct," Mrs. Kalustian said and fastened her arm around Flora. She turned toward Mrs. Adamian. "Did you say you were leaving?"

"Oh, good," Mihran said. "I am, too. I'll walk you home."

Face flushed, Mrs. Adamian rose to leave. "Visit us soon, Flora. Dinner tomorrow evening?"

Flora shook her head. "Not tomorrow."

"Let me know when, dear, dear, Flora." She kissed Flora's cheeks and left with Mihran.

Hearing a sigh of relief, Flora turned to see a smiling Mrs. Kalustian comfortable in the overstuffed chair.

When one wants you, everyone does, Flora chuckled to herself as she approached the woman. I wonder which son she's going to offer.

"Now, Mrs. Kalustian, what did you say you wanted?"

FORTY ONE

SEPARATION

The news about Flora's virginity spread rapidly within the Hadjin community. Five more ladies with marriageable sons came to visit, all trying to woo Flora away from her decision to marry the young Armenian from America. They all said the same thing… You don't know anything about him. Who'll protect you in that foreign country? You should stay here and marry a Hadjin boy.

But Flora had made up her mind. Sarkis Ketlegian offered her a new life, and she was determined to take it. She also knew that Khatoon Ketlegian was just as determined not to let a Hadjin mother steal her away. Daily, the woman kept her abreast of their travel plans. But Flora knew those visits were designed to keep her focused on Sarkis, like dangling a carrot in front of a rabbit. Their meetings together were always warm and congenial, and Flora had grown to like her. She poured out her heart to the responsive woman. How could Khatoon not know she was already a willing rabbit?

The only sad moment came when Mrs. Ketlegian told her the chances of sponsoring Verkin and Mihran were unlikely. Even though Sarkis had attended the missionary college in Talas, his Turkish education was not useful in America. He was merely a factory worker. And he still had to fund passage for his two brothers and Berjoohy.

When Flora told her sister and uncle the bad news, she was surprised by their response. Both understood. They seemed to have resigned themselves to whatever their fate might be.

"Uncle, let's give Flora a new wardrobe… a wedding present," Verkin said. "Hrant and his parents will give me the fabrics, if I ask them. I can design the dresses, and you can sew them."

"Good idea," Mihran responded. "But, not too many, now."

"Three outfits?" Verkin asked.

Mihran nodded. "That will be fine."

Since that eventful afternoon when the mid-wife had confirmed her virginity, Flora noticed that Mihran had softened his attitude toward her. He was showing her his gentler side, and she found herself actually liking him... something she had never thought possible.

* * *

The days that followed were joyful. Verkin draped linens, cottons, silks and lightweight black serge around Flora, who stood in front of the one tall mirror in the fabric shop. Many of the fabrics were black or white or had black and white designs. They were the popular colors of the day.

Flora reached for the white linen bolt filled with tiny black polka dots. "A dress?"

Verkin nodded, took Flora's measurements, cut the material, and pinned the cut pieces on her sister. The line of the dress was simple, but lovely. With its low waist, fitted arms and pleated skirt that reached her ankles, Flora knew the dress would have a flowing movement when she walked. She watched as Verkin attached three rows of narrow black ribbon just above the bottom of the skirt. Then Verkin wrapped a one inch black ribbon around the dress, just below her breasts.

"To emphasize your assets," Verkin pushed up Flora's breasts. "Hmmm. We better fit you with a new brassiere, too."

Next, Verkin fitted Flora with white cotton for a blouse with matching lace around the neckline and wrists. The skirt would be black and ankle length, but as yet, Verkin hadn't decided upon which fabric. Maybe linen.

"Flora, maybe we should also make you a new coat. It can get cold out there in the middle of the ocean."

The words jolted her. The middle of the ocean... she'd be leaving soon... before Verkin's child was born... never to hold the newborn or ever again hug her sister. The thought was almost too much to bear. Then the incomprehensible crossed her mind, and she blurted out, "What if things go terribly wrong with Sarkis?"

"Nothing will go wrong, little sister." Verkin stroked Flora's hair. "And if they do, Antranig is in New York. And Siran and Krikor should be there by now too." She patted her growing belly and laughed. "With God's blessing, your time will come... and maybe sooner than you think."

Overcome, Flora grasped Verkin and hugged her, not wanting to let go. "I'm going to miss you."

"Ouch." Verkin backed away and removed a pin that had jabbed one of her full breasts. Flora was still pinned into the white blouse.

* * *

Wearing her newly made blouse and black linen skirt, her wide brimmed hat, the white now accented with a rib of black silk and two long, poufy black feathers, Flora stood on the wooden platform of the Adana train station. She said her bittersweet good-byes.

Mrs. Ketlegian looked distressed as she hugged Berjoohy and her sons good-bye. The day had arrived—June 1, 1920—Flora and her future mother-in-law were leaving Turkey for good.

They boarded the train for Constantinople and quickly found their seats in the second class compartment. Flora pressed her face against the window, watching Verkin, Uncle Mihran, Auntie, Hrant and his parents. As the train pulled out of the station her longing eyes lingered on Verkin, still searching long after Verkin was out of view.

Her foot, with its high button, black leather shoe, brushed against the strong straw basket she hadn't yet stored away. She chose to use the new basket in preference to an old battered suitcase her uncle had offered. Inside she had packed the new black pumps Mihran had given her, Miss Webb's Bible, her necessities and all of her new clothes—the black, double breasted serge coat, the polka dot dress Verkin had made in two separate pieces, so she could mix and match with the blouse and skirt she now wore. She had also packed the black and white checkered dress Mr. Plato's wife had given her, and the petticoat she hadn't worn since the day of General Allenby's celebration.

She was ready to impress America.

FORTY-TWO

A NEW ADMIRER

The wheels screeched as the train pulled into the Constantinople station. The sounds triggered memories. Bittersweet. Her wonderful Miss Webb... the exciting days at the college... the American embassy parties... her hopes and dreams and those of her friends, Ana and Sona... the poor souls... were they still alive?

"Quickly, quickly." Khatoon hurried Flora off the train and rushed her through the station that reeked of cigarette smoke. The older woman pushed past the crowds and out the station's stained glass double doors. She waved to the closest cabbie. His horses stood quietly, waiting. "Galata Bridge. To the wharf," Khatoon said as she and Flora climbed into the closed carriage.

The Constantinople streets thrived as people went about their business in the warm afternoon. But Flora felt something missing. Turkish men no longer walked with long strides nor did their faces carry the confidence she had previously witnessed. The war had changed them.

The carriage pulled up at the wharf where a wide, dilapidated ferry was taking on passengers. Smells of fried fish hung in the air. Restaurants and hawkers were selling the morning catch of the local fishermen.

Khatoon paid the driver while Flora waited by the ferry's gangplank. Men boarding noticed her and smiled. Had her new fashions attracted them or did they think she was pretty? Regardless, Flora liked the attention. She could easily get used to her new image.

"Quickly." Khatoon hurried her onto the ferry that was to take them to Greece, where in two days they were to board the Greek ocean liner, *Megali Hellas*. Descending to the middle deck, they found their second class cabin and settled in. Pushing the baggage under the bunk bed that filled the cramped room, Flora began to feel closed in. "I think I'll go outside for a while."

Khatoon slumped onto the lower bunk. "Not me. I'm going to rest."

Flora quietly closed the door behind her, stood on the deck and breathed in the salt air. The lumbering boat steamed out of the harbor as the sun fell toward the horizon. Rays of golden light sparkled and bounced off the water like a glittering cornucopia. Now she understood why the harbor was called the Golden Horn.

There in front of her was Stamboul, the oldest and most picturesque part of Constantinople with it minarets reaching up to the heavens. She looked for the embassy and the college and couldn't see them, but she knew they were there, as real as the wonderful memories—the camaraderie, the elegance of the embassy parties, the learning—they would be with her forever.

The ancient city began to fade in the twilight. Turkey would no longer be part of her life. Could the horrific memories of the recent years fade as easily? The world she wanted so desperately was gone. Her pained heart was a constant reminder of better times. Her eyes welled. She longed to feel secure again. Oh, how she missed her family, especially her father. And now Sarkis, this man she knew only in a photograph, was coming into her life. Would he protect and care for her as did her beloved father? She didn't dare think beyond that thought, but she had memorized Antranig's address in New York... just in case. Her new life was filled with uncertainty.

Bracing her hands on the rail as the ship entered the rougher waters of the Sea of Marmara, she felt a breeze and placed her hand on top of her hat before it blew away.

"Nice time of evening," said the young man who approached and stood next to her.

"Yes, it is." But Flora didn't feel like talking at this particular moment.

"You're Armenian?" he asked.

She nodded and took off her hat. She felt silly standing there with her hand on top of her head.

"Will you be staying in Greece?" he asked.

"Just long enough to board the *Megali Hellas*."

"Ahhh. So, you're going to America too."

"Yes." A strong breeze whipped across her face and blew her hair to one side. She pulled it forward so her curly ends rested just below her shoulder. Then she took a good look at the young man whose keen brown eyes were searching hers for reaction.

"You're not married?" he asked.

"Engaged."

"Oh," he sighed.

A familiar voice called, "Flora!"

She turned to see Khatoon standing by the cabin door, concern written all over her face. "My future mother-in-law," she whispered to the disappointed-looking young man.

"Come inside, Flora. I don't want you catching cold."

She nodded and watched the young Armenian walk slowly away.

"Who is he?"

"I don't know. We didn't talk much. I just know he's Armenian." She decided it best not to mention that the young man was also on his way to America... and on the same boat.

FORTY-THREE

A DEFLATING OFFER

The ferryboat swayed throughout the night, steaming southward toward its first stop. But as morning approached, the winds grew heavy and the boat heaved through the rougher waters of the Aegean. Finally, it slowed, the engines stopped, and the anchor dropped with a heavy splash.

Flora opened her eyes to see light filtering through the cabin's small porthole.

"We're in Smyrna," Khatoon said.

Flora pulled the blanket over her head.

"*Aghchig,* (girl) what's the matter?"

"Ohhh."

"Are you seasick?"

"Ohhhh."

"I'll get hot tea."

Flora heard the cabin door close. She wanted to see Smyrna's famous waterfront, but when she lifted her head, the room began to swirl. Carefully lowering herself from the top bunk, she ran to the toilet, vomited and dragged herself back to bed.

An hour later when the ship pulled out of the harbor, Flora heard the boat's feeble horn toot. She drew her knees up to her chest. The rough day continued, and she felt so terrible she thought she might die. Finally, the waters calmed. She fell asleep and didn't wake till the next morning.

Opening her eyes, she saw Khatoon holding a loaf of crusty bread. She reached out for a piece.

"You feeling better?"

She nodded and managed to hold down the bread and a hard boiled egg, some of the foodstuffs Khatoon had packed for the trip.

"We should be docking in three hours or so." Khatoon rearranged things in her suitcase. "When you're ready, we'll go upstairs."

"Upstairs?"

"Yes. There is a food stall where the tea is cheap."

Flora understood. The once wealthy woman had to stretch what little money she now had.

The open upper deck was filled with third-class passengers wrapped in blankets or heavy coats and sitting or lying on the wooden benches where they had spent the night. Flora buttoned her coat. The early morning air was chilly.

"Sit here and wait," Khatoon said. "I'll bring the tea."

Flora sat on the empty bench, waited, and when Khatoon arrived they sat together quietly sipping the hot tea. She listened to the sounds of the boat slicing its way through the water. Suddenly she had a peculiar feeling. She lifted her head to see the young Armenian. His keen eyes had focused on her.

Not wanting to encourage him, she lowered her eyes. Had he been searching for her? He looked much stronger than the young men she knew who had survived the exile. Was he from Constantinople? For some unknown reason many Armenians in Constantinople and Smyrna had not been deported.

When she looked up again, he was gone.

* * *

At last the rugged coastline of Greece came into view. Flora caught a glimpse of the Acropolis standing high above Athens. The ruins of the once magnificent city grew smaller and smaller as the ferryboat chugged on to the Greek port of Piraeus, another twelve miles away. So close, yet so far. She'd never breathe the air of that grand history. Then, a powerful insight struck her. She had to let go of her own past in order to move on. Adrenaline surged through her body as she saw the faces of her parents. Would she do them a disservice by letting them go? They were still too much a part of her life, for she thought of them every day and the pain of the exile never left her, not even for a day.

The memory of her parents began to fade as she set her legs on the Piraeus wharf. Her eyes fell on the sleek black ocean liner anchored in the harbor. Mammoth white letters spelled its name: M E G A L I H E L L A S. She hoped the handsome new boat would be steadier on the water than the aged Greek ferryboat from which she had just disembarked.

"Hurry, Flora. I want to confirm our cabin reservations and make our appointments with the doctor."

She followed Khatoon into the steamship office where paper and trash littered the floor at the feet of a hundred anxious emigrants. Paint was peeling from the walls. Yellowish light from hanging ceiling lights filtered through thick cigarette smoke. Smells of unwashed bodies, stale foods and garlic disturbed her delicate stomach.

Khatoon set her luggage on the dirty floor. "Stay here."

"Can I wait outside? It's too close in here."

"Yes... but near the entrance." Khatoon rushed to find a place in the growing line.

Flora picked up their two pieces of baggage.

"Can I help you?"

Hearing his pleasant voice, Flora turned to see the young Armenian.

Lifting her basket he walked outside, his own suitcase in his other hand.

He must have overheard our conversation, she thought, but why hadn't she seen him? Should that worry her? That he might be watching her all the way to America?

"Are you staying in New York?" he asked and set down the luggage.

Hesitating, she finally answered, "Boston." She wasn't sure she should be talking to him.

"I hope you don't think I'm too bold." His keen eyes were intent, but not threatening.

"My older brother lives in New York," he continued, "and he wants very much to marry a nice Armenian girl."

Flora felt her ego deflating. He wasn't interested in her after all.

"There aren't many Armenian girls in America. Wish there were more... especially as pretty as you... and with those lovely green eyes of yours."

He made her feel as if she were a prize. Her ego now recovered, she thanked him and gently reconfirmed her betrothal to the Bostonian.

They talked and Flora learned that he was from Constantinople and hoped to become a notable doctor. His brother, a poet by night and a tailor by day, had paid for his passage and had made arrangements for him to attend college in New York.

A college education! That, too, had been her dream.

"Flora!" Khatoon's voice was harsh. The woman had fire in her eyes as she ran toward the startled couple.

"*Parev* (Hello)." He nodded to Khatoon. "I'd better get in line to confirm my reservation." He picked up his bag.

Khatoon's eyes followed him until he disappeared inside the building. Then she snapped, "What did he want?"

Flora didn't know how to answer. She hadn't seen this contemptuous side of Khatoon and felt unnerved.

"What did he want?" Khatoon snapped again.

Flora blurted out. "He wanted to know if I'd consider marrying his brother."

"I knew it! As soon as I saw him. I knew he'd try to steal you away from me and my Sarkis."

Flora gently placed her hand on Khatoon's arm. "Please trust me. You've given me the hope I never thought I'd find again. I'd never betray you... or Sarkis, my betrothed."

"Oh, my sweet dear girl." Khatoon hugged and squeezed her so tightly Flora could hardly breathe.

She was amazed that Khatoon, this older woman who survived three years of hell in the barren desert, could be so strong.

FORTY-FOUR

THE *MEGALI HELLAS*

After a night's rest in a nearby travelers hotel, Flora and Khatoon stood on the dock with more than a thousand other third class passengers, all waiting patiently to board the ocean liner embarking for New York on her maiden voyage.

A heavy mist hung over the harbor. The outline of the sleek passenger ship faded only to reappear as the mist lifted.

As one hundred twenty first class passengers were escorted up the gangplank, the expression on Khatoon's face saddened. Flora understood. In ordinary times Khatoon would have been traveling with them. Then the eighty cabin class passengers were escorted onto the ship.

Finally, their turn came. But no escorts. Greek stewards directed the masses of immigrants to the lower decks where dormitory style rooms with bunk beds awaited them.

Having bribed her Greek agent for good accommodations, Khatoon handed a steward several Greek coins and their passage tickets. He took them down to the third deck and opened the door of Cabin 3234. Inside, a Greek woman with three young children had already claimed two of the three bunks. They introduced themselves as Flora pushed her baggage under the remaining bunk.

The ship began its maneuver away from the dock. "I'm going out on deck," Flora said to Khatoon.

"I'll come, too."

The forward deck was crowded with passengers, many leaning against the ship's rail. Waving and shouting to forlorn family and friends standing on the dock, the Greek emigrants' joyous faces said it all. They were embarking for America, a land they hoped would give them a better life. There they stayed until the dock had disappeared into the horizon.

We are so lucky, Flora thought, until she overhead a woman say to her companion, "My friend said seasoned passengers shy away from maiden voyages until a ship proves that everything on board works and can safely cross the ocean. Oh God, I hope we don't sink like the *Titanic* did."

The remark startled Flora. Should she be concerned? She'd heard the Atlantic Ocean could become cruel in violent storms. But as darkness descended and the ship blazed with electric lights and heat warmed the dining hall, Flora knew the newly built *Megali Hellas* would take her safely to America.

Waiting her turn in the cafeteria line for dinner, Flora smiled as she noticed the young Armenian sitting in the crowded dining area. An attractive dark-haired teenage girl sat across from him. Hmmm. Would this girl become his brother's bride?

Not wanting to upset her future mother-in-law again, Flora decided she would avoid the young man for the entire trip, interesting as he was. He reminded her of her brother, Levon, who also had planned to study medicine. Dear, dear, Levon. Her eyes became teary. How could she let go of her family? Her memories were painfully deep.

After dinner she and Khatoon stood together on the bow. The night was crisp and clear. Brilliant stars twinkled and gave Flora an eerie, but calming feeling. Were they flashing her a message about her family?

Searching the heavens, she thought of her father, mother, brothers and Nubar, who had sacrificed his life so she and Verkin could escape. Were they in the arms of the Divine Father?

And what of Miss Webb?

That night before dropping off to sleep, Flora opened her Bible. Her eyes fell on the inscription Miss Webb's preacher father had written... *May God always bestow his blessings unto you, my dear daughter, who has chosen to dedicate her life to Him....*

Dedicating her life to Him. Yes, indeed. That's what Miss Webb had done. Flora hoped her wonderful teacher was in heaven, comforted and sitting on the lap of the Divine Father.

FORTY-FIVE

NEW YORK

Sixteen days later the *Megali Hellas* entered the narrows of New York Harbor. The third-class forward deck was crammed with expectant immigrants dressed in shawls and overcoats, their heads covered with hats and scarves. The morning air was chilly.

There was a palpable silence on the deck as the Manhattan skyline came into view. Scores of ferryboats and steamships flying flags of many nations were docked at the Hudson River pier. The Statue of Liberty, her torch uplifted toward the heavens, rose like a welcoming benefactor giving the newly arriving Greek ship and her passengers a blessing. Memories of smelly unwashed bodies and odors of seasickness faded quickly.

Standing next to Khatoon, Flora heard the man standing behind her address the mighty woman with the torch… "Thank you Mother of Exiles. I am tired and poor, and I yearn to breathe free." Flora turned to see a middle aged man bundled in a frayed coat, his damp eyes radiant.

But she felt anxious. Her eyes scanned the ominous, red brick buildings of Ellis Island that stood in the shadow of the noble statue. There lay the new immigrants' greatest fear—deportation. She'd heard stories of how some families had to make painful decisions right on the spot whether to go back on the returning boat with a rejected loved one, or stay in this new land and send the loved one back alone. She thought of the Greek lady in her cabin. What if one of her children was rejected? Would she leave the other two children with her Greek American husband and return to Greece with the rejected child? What if the woman was rejected? That fearful thought also struck her. What if she was deported? What would she do in Greece, alone and with no money? She shuddered.

An announcement came from the Captain. "First class passengers may disembark."

"Lucky," Khatoon said watching the first and then the cabin class passengers walk down the gangplank. Their visit through customs would be quick.

Their turn finally came. A deckhand shouting through a megaphone announced, "Third class passengers are required to board the waiting ferries."

Flora's eyes again fell on the red brick buildings. That's where the ferries would take her and the others. Just down the river her future was about to unfold. She felt the lump in her throat tighten.

Khatoon grasped Flora's hand and pulled her toward the gangplank, thick with new immigrants rushing to board the ferries. "I don't want to lose you, especially now."

"I won't let you out of my sight, not for a moment," Flora blurted out and hurried to follow the woman onto an already crowded ferry. Giving their baggage to a deck hand to store, they climbed stairs to the upper deck and watched their approach to the island.

Fifteen minutes later they joined masses of immigrants laden with bundles, baggage and children stepping off the boat and were immediately greeted with shouts and commands. Men herded them into lines and pinned numbered tags on the new immigrants. Now they had to wait to pass the tests that would allow them to enter America.

"Let me do the talking," Khatoon said. "Remember, you are my daughter... when they ask you who you are."

Flora nodded. She wouldn't forget. All the way across the ocean she had studied her betrothed's photograph and mentally practiced her new name. Sarkis' face held a kindness that had already reached into her heart.

Three hours passed before Flora and Khatoon stood in front of a doctor. They knew what he was looking for. More than half the medical detentions were for eye infections, especially trachoma. "You, first," he said to Flora.

He lifted her eyelids and searched underneath for infection. It hurt, but Flora didn't dare move or say anything.

"Please take off your hat" he said, waited till she removed it, and looked through her hair, pressing places around her neck and checking over her hands. "Move on. You're clear."

Relieved, Flora waited as the doctor examined Khatoon. She breathed another sigh of relief when she heard him tell her to move on.

Now, one more inspection to pass. The most important one. This large bellied man held the treasured landing cards. He would decide if they could stay in America. "Who paid for your ship's fare?" he asked, as if he was bored.

Khatoon quickly replied, "My son. He lives in Boston." She grasped Flora's hand. "My daughter. He paid for both of us."

He asked twenty-eight more questions... "Can you read and write?...Who is meeting you?... Where are you going?... How much money do you have?... Where did you get it?... Show it to me...."

Satisfied with the answers, he handed Khatoon and Flora their cards. "Welcome to your new home."

"Thank you," Khatoon said. She hugged Flora. "Quickly. Let's find Sarkis."

"Wait!" Flora placed her white hat on her head. "Do I look alright?"

"*Yavrum*, you're lovely. My Sarkis will love you just as you are."

The happy pair flew through the swinging doors and raced down the stairs to the reception room where new immigrants met their loved ones. Filled with joy, wives and children kissed and hugged their husbands and fathers, while grown men let tears flow. Those who were not met by friends or relatives waited in groups where a guide would take them to the appropriate train or bus station.

Flora saw his familiar face. He looked exactly like the image in the photograph. Wearing a light brown suit, Sarkis sat in a chair, a book in his hand. When he saw Khatoon, he sprang from the chair, ran and embraced his mother with a son's tender affection.

Surprised at his height, Flora had expected Sarkis to be not much taller than her five feet.

Khatoon turned to Flora. "This is my boy, Sarkis."

Nearly six inches taller than she, he took her hand. "Welcome." His smile was warm. "You're even prettier than my mother said."

She liked his affable voice. Her heart soared.

He handed the book to his mother. Flora delighted as she noted the title—Thoreau, *The Poet-Naturalist.*

"I have something for you." Sarkis reached into his pocket and brought out a small, red velvet box. Opening it, he removed a gold ring with a small blue stone and slipped it on Flora's finger. It fit perfectly.

"It's beautiful." Flora kissed the ring and held back her tears. She had never before owned a piece of jewelry. Gazing into his gentle brown eyes, she sensed that same kindness she had seen in the photograph. He was more than she had hoped for.

Sarkis took Flora's hand again, linked his arm through his mother's, and led them to the door that would launch their new lives. Suddenly Flora felt a sense of freedom she hadn't imagined possible.

As Sarkis opened the door, a ray of sunshine, reddish like that of the sun reflecting off a piece of crystal, sparkled on his hair.

Flora noticed his face glow and could almost feel Grandmother Shushan smiling down at her and whispering, "He's a gift in the sunlight."

And three apples fell down from heaven
one for the storyteller
one for the listener
And one for those who never give up hope

EPILOGUE

The roots of *A Gift in the Sunlight* grew from stories my mother, Flora, told me. But I really wrote this story because remarkable things happened to my mother in her elder years. She died in 1989, should have died in 1984, and I'd like to tell you about those extraordinary five years, because it is the story behind the story.

Flora was hospitalized in 1984 at age 83, having outlived her husband and two of her four children. She was terminally ill with congestive heart failure, had severe hand tremors and couldn't feed herself. Confused, she had forgotten people she once knew, probably due to the onset of Alzheimer's.

"Let her spend her last few days at home," her doctor said.

With a heavy heart, I brought her home. Her final moments were near, and I did not expect her to survive the night. But I was wrong. Flora slowly began to recover. Within three months her hand tremors subsided completely. More amazingly, she was again clear and alert, as if her brain cells had been revitalized.

I didn't know what to think. I watched as she developed new relationships with friends that only recently she hadn't recognized. She couldn't resurface those past associations, but she remembered everything about them from then on—as if she met them for the first time.

And something else even more wonderful happened. My mother had become more loving!

Until now, her life had been shadowed by the Armenian tragedy. She was filled with anger and self-pity and dwelt on the horrors of the past. She often talked about her family who had perished at the hands of the Turks. Now, incredibly, that dark shadow was *gone*. Something was happening inside Flora's heart, something beyond my ability to understand. But I do remember telling friends, in humble humor, that she left her negative qualities on the other side and came back with all of her good qualities intensified! Today I smile when I think that transmutation may have actually occurred.

My mother had three more near death crises where we, the family, were told she couldn't survive without the help of a respirator. In each case we refused, feeling she needed to move on if it was her time. But each time Flora came home to die, she slowly began to recover. And with each recovery she became more *alert* and more *loving*. Even her doctor began to refer to her as "the miracle lady."

I feel privileged to have been a witness to her amazing transformation, but I was also awed. As her primary caregiver, there were times she was so frail I couldn't leave her side for even two minutes. Every time she came home from the hospital in those deathly states, her needs were constant. There were times she didn't have the strength to even move her head without help. Then, within two or three months, she was strong enough to once again attend her church and senior citizen activities.

I was puzzled, but happy these wonderful things were happening to my mother. I would have expected coming as close to death as often as she did that her brain cells would have atrophied instead of being revived. And to see her walk again, without help, human or mechanical, was absolutely amazing.

But it was her fourth encounter with death that really stopped me. In 1988, when Flora was in one of her strong modes, I went to Aleppo to search for the Plato Sawaides family. The day after I found the one remaining descendant, a daughter born two years after my mother left Aleppo, I received a call from home. Flora was back in the hospital. I left for Los Angeles.

When I saw my mother on that hospital bed, I was sure this time her time had come. She tried to smile, but was too weak. "I don't know why I didn't die" she said, her voice barely audible.

And I, too, wondered. Did she know something I didn't? I leaned close. "Mom, do you think you will die now?"

"It doesn't look like it," she said, her voice cracking and her face reflecting her own disbelief.

Somehow, she knew.

Two days later when I entered cardiac care, I was surprised to see my mother sitting up in bed, unattended. The day before she couldn't even turn her head without help. But when she saw me she shouted something in Turkish, a language she hadn't spoken in more than fifty years!

I was startled. She was filled with energy. And why was she speaking Turkish? "Mom, I don't understand you," I said, trying to calm her. "Speak to me in English or Armenian."

She kept shouting in Turkish, and I began to panic. What if she continued to speak only Turkish? Would I lose contact with her forever?

"Mom," I said firmly, wondering if I could retrain her brain to think in English. "Repeat everything I say." I went through the entire English alphabet. She repeated each letter dutifully, as if she were in school following a teacher's instructions. We counted numbers and she repeated those in English. But then she started to shout in Turkish again. An occasional English or Armenian word was in the mix. I struggled to understand. The best I could comprehend was the following:

"They took my education!" she yelled.

"They took my family! Do you know what it was like? I went crazy!"

Then, she looked straight into my eyes, and said loud and clear in *English*.

"THE BASTARDS!"

I couldn't hold back a laugh. Moments ago I was panicking, but this boisterous comment was just plain comical. And throughout this wild scenario, even when she was shouting in Turkish, she appeared joyful.

"Mom, are you happy?" I asked trying to understand this bizarre phenomenon.

"Yes," came the *emphatic* reply.

"Why?"

"Because I'm awake!" she said with authority.

I found her choice of word intriguing. I would have expected her to say, "Because I'm alive." But after three recoveries from what I now call, *her return from death's door*, I had a suspicion of what might have happened. Could she have crossed over into another plane and witnessed the Armenian Holocaust from a higher, non personal view? Had she gained insight into the horrific karmic debt the perpetrators have to pay? And had she been given an opportunity to release her own intense hatred of the Turk? Was that hatred released with the strong expulsion of her anger as she shouted, THE BASTARDS, a word not in my old-fashioned mother's vocabulary? I'll never know for sure, but I can state for a fact that Flora was so loving after this fourth brush with death that she couldn't harbor hatred, not even toward the Turks. Love poured out of her heart, like a flower releasing its perfume. Everyone around her felt it.

But this was not the only unusual episode during my mother's long illness. Her second bout with congestive heart failure in 1986 was also a stunner. With her heart laboring in cardiac care, her doctor didn't expect her to survive the night. Three of us sat at her bedside, waiting. Flora had been unresponsive. Then she started to speak.

"Do you know why I'm still here?" she asked, sounding as if she knew a great truth. She looked at my cousin and said, "Because you don't have any children." She turned toward me and again said, "You don't have any children." Then she spotted my nephew sitting a little further away and said, "And you don't have any children. If I died, no one would know."

"They showed me a lot of pictures," she continued.

I wondered who the "they" were. I knew people with near death experiences claimed to view their lives at the moment of death. Was my mother sharing the same kind of "vision" with whomever the "they" were?

She looked at my cousin. "Your mother was there." His mother had died some thirty years prior. She named others, particularly an Armenian family who was a karmic mirror of her own family and told us prophetic things that would happen to members of our own family. Two of them have already come to pass.

"They showed the afghans," she said. She'd made afghans for everyone over the years, relatives, neighbors, my friends, her friends, and my sister's friends. Interestingly, after this "vision" she made them specifically for disabled veterans. I think she was extending her newly kindled understanding and love to those who also had been through the hell of war.

She turned her gaze to me. "You're going to write a book about my life."

"No, Mom, not me," I responded. "Maybe your other daughter will. She's the real Armenian in the family."

"No, you are, and you're going to be on the Donahue show."

The Donahue Show! In 1986 Donahue was the king of talk shows, and she never, but never, watched that program. I immediately brushed off that statement as nonsense.

Then she ended her little speech with, "They said it was my choice." Now, that sentence gripped my attention. I've spent my adult life trying to make right choices, and it is not ever an easy thing. Now my mother said she had made the choice to stay on in defiance of her body's deathly state. She had more to do before she could let go. I just didn't know it at the time.

Against the odds, she rallied and a few days later she was released from the hospital. In the middle of her first night home, I heard her stir. I rushed into her bedroom and turned on the light. There she sat in bed, her face radiant.

She gave me a huge smile and said, *"Do you know what life is all about?"* Not waiting for a reply, she said, *"It's all about love and understanding, but everyone's brain is not the same, so you help when you can. That's what life's all about!"* She smiled again, laid herself down, and went back to sleep.

I will never forget that night.

The next day she again couldn't move without help.

I had dismissed much of her "vision" on that hospital bed as delusion, particularly the part about Donahue. I certainly had no plans to write a book about her or the Armenian tragedy. My mind was focused on researching material for exercises that stimulate the body's "chi", and I had been accepted to study at the Acupuncture International Training Centre in Beijing, China. But what was happening to my mother was remarkable, and I was deeply affected. I began to read about events that happened in the Ottoman Empire during World War I. I became overwhelmed. I had not known the depth of the Armenian tragedy, and I began to understand the heartbreaking scars on my mother's heart and on the hearts of Armenian survivors everywhere. Now I knew that my mother's story needed to be told, the whole of it, including the blessing that was granted her in her last years. Having no idea how difficult that would be, I set aside my plans to study in China to write Flora's story.

If her story has heart, and if by some miracle I actually do appear on a Donahue type show as she prophesized back in 1986, what message did this little woman, who kept escaping death and instead became more alert and more loving each time, really have to tell?

END

TADERON PRESS

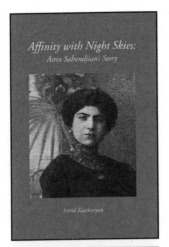

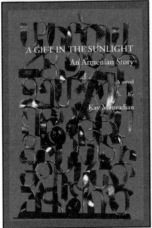

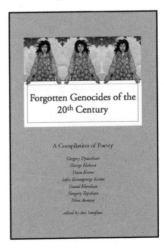

ABOUT THE AUTHOR:

Dr. Mouradian is a retired Professor of Health and Physical Education. Her publications include *Reflective Meditation, A Mind Calming Technique* (Theosophical Pub. House, 1982) as well as a number of articles.

Dr. Mouradian wrote *A Gift in the Sunlight* after her mother's remarkable recoveries from death's door prompted her to examine her own ancestral past. After working in various libraries and archives in the United States, Dr. Mouradian visited the village where her mother and her mother's family, along with 20,000 other Armenians, were forced to leave their homes. Traveling across the same deportation route where more than a million Armenians were forced to march during the Armenian Genocide, she became acutely aware of the suffering of her mother's generation and the lingering sense of injustice they carried.

Dr. Mouradian, who has started a new career as a writer, hopes her novel will provide a platform for reconciliation through understanding and compassion.

ETHNIC HATRED

breeds
and
begets

rape
sadism
duress
cruelty
suffering
homelessness
brutality
and
bestiality

and the end result is

ORPHANS